The Ivory Tower

Duchess MacKinnon

Dedication

I believe this may be the hardest dedication I will ever write because the wealth of emotion attached to this person is almost indescribable and I struggle with the words. This dedication is for my Aunt Marion. It takes a village to raise a child and she was part of my village. She lived with my family for a couple of years. Or at least it felt that way! She was a massive thorn in my side, and I loved every second of it. When she moved back to Florida, I was heartbroken. This book is about the discovery of family and she is part of the foundation for ours. She helped keep her family together when she was only sixteen years old. She is a mother, grandmother, great grandmother, and great-great grandmother. She taught me so many things growing up about family and being resilient against the stings and arrows of outrageous fortune. If I keep at it, just telling you stories about her, I would easily wrack up several thousand more words. What I can say is she is beloved of many and most especially by me. Aunt Marion, this one is for you.

Chapter One - Allison

I took a deep breath to try and steady my nerves. If someone had asked me if I would have been demanding a private meeting with Renaldo Corsetti, the vampire king of Chicago three short months ago, I would have thought it a fine joke and laughed. Unfortunately, it wasn't a fine joke. It was my birthday when my world changed and everything, I had ever dreamed for disappeared. My father who had been a sporadic presence in my life had come to visit me. He always made sure he saw me on my birthday. Most years it was uneventful. This year, however, was definitely not the same.

My father is the Reverend James Monroe. We had already had several disagreements because I loathed his cause. Unfortunately, he leads one of the largest hate groups against the vampires, shapeshifters, and anyone else that is different called Humans Only. Oh, he disguises it under a church description but let's be honest. A spade is a spade even if you call it a pitchfork. We obviously didn't agree which caused a few fights. He didn't approve of my liberal thoughts on the world. In fact, I don't think there isn't anything about me that he really approved of or agreed with. We argued over high school electives, my clothes, and he didn't like my choice to do only a two-year degree in business.

However, at the end of the day it was my life and once I turned 18, he couldn't really stop me. When he threatened to cut me off financially, I shrugged and told him it was his prerogative to do as he wished. While I understood that his daughter from his "other family" was killed because of the monsters that did not make them all evil. At least I used to think he had a reason that I could understand. Then suddenly, I discovered that I should be grateful I wasn't dead. Dead by his own hand. I was also very relieved that I never confided in him some of my oddities. He seemed to know though.

It turned out that he had kept a number of things from me over the years. Apparently, I had a sister and she was none other than Cassandra James, formerly known as Alyssa Monroe. He forgot to tell her about me too. I wasn't completely special in the secret department. I was also pretty sure his wife didn't know these things either. Though I had heard things weren't going so well there. I didn't believe it at first. However, why lie? I did do some research in the family tree. His story did kind of makes some sense. He suggested I go knock on her door, say, "Surprise you have a sister now teach me everything you know." Okay I am over dramatizing the verbal statements. It would be essentially the same thing.

I was excellent at research and decided to go to the one source that had truly studied my newly discovered sister and what she was all about. The vampire who was her primary adversary. Now I know that might not seem to make sense. But since I never really thought my father a friend and a bit of a nuisance, I knew almost everything I could find about him. I figured that the vampire king of Chicago would have that same devotion. It also helped that in the smallest recess of my mind that when I told my father it would send him into a rage of epic proportions. Which would be good. He deserved it. I had never been a rebellious child. Enough was enough though.

I admit I almost lost courage when the cab stopped in front of the very imposing Ivory Tower, the lair of Chicago's bad guy. It really was a bit of the way it was described. It was a large, tall building. But unlike the other buildings that were a varying shade of dark colors, steel, and glass, the Ivory tower was an imposing white building.

The person who met me was a big, burly guy in a black suit. All he needed was the sunglasses and he would have the perfect men in black costume. He certainly perfected the haute couture mafia look. He of course told me I was shit out of luck. Again, I am being overly dramatic. The master was not in. That I had to make an appointment and that would take months. Afterall, his lordship was a very busy man. Given that I didn't have months to wait I did the only self-respecting thing that his world would understand. I bribed him.

Apparently, it worked after he recovered from the shock of the girl in Sunday School haute couture coolly bribing him as if this was something, I did every day. He smiled and said, "For a grand I can make a lot of things happen."

"I thought you might," I said dryly.

Chapter Two - Renaldo

I leaned back in my chair and peered across the desk and assessed Bruce who started to squirm just a bit. I wasn't angry at him. In fact, I was rather surprised that he would accept a bribe which left me a mental note to check out what was going on in his life to be buyable. Though, who knew. He might have had a soft spot for innocent girls. Maybe she reminded him of his favorite sister.

"Let me understand this correctly. You have arranged for me to meet a wisp of a girl who is obviously the most innocent looking pathological liar into my presence because she claims to be Cassandra James's sister and you did so on the back of a thousand dollars? Did you realize I have never found any evidence that Cassandra has any living family and if she did, I would have known about them wouldn't I? Did you get the money upfront?"

Bruce rolled his eyes. "To answer your questions, yes, yes, and yes." Bruce patted his breast pocket that did bulge slightly. Of course, he would. One thing I instilled in all my men was to value of the deal and it didn't exist until the transaction was made. It's just that their side deals never involved me personally.

"Tell me this, why? You're not the one that typically can be bought." Bruce squirmed a bit more.

"I need the money," he said lowly, but he knew I could hear him.

"Do I need to give you a raise?" He brightened a bit at that.

"With health insurance?" My eyes narrowed. He went furry once a month and bayed at the moon. What in the hell would he do with health insurance? Shapeshifters don't get sick.

"I suppose I could arrange that, but you don't get sick."

Bruce squirmed a little more. "I knocked a girl up." He said really fast.

"You're sure it's yours?" I winced internally. Gads I was cynical. Even Cassandra was right about that.

"Of course, I am one hundred percent sure. I want to marry her. She's holding out on me with that. She doesn't really like who I work for."

I shook my head. I really hadn't been paying attention. "How long have you been going out?"

"Over a year."

Oh yeah, I needed to really keep a closer eye on my house. I was getting sloppy. I hadn't been the same since Cassandra James had left town. She posed a real threat to me and kept me on edge.

"Congratulations, go ahead and bring the girl in."

"Master?"

"Yes?"

"Don't frighten her too much. She's really a tiny little thing and well she does look kind of like Cassandra. She might really be as lethal." Oh yeah. Bruce never really thought Cassandra was much of a threat. Then she killed my best fighters. When the first one died everyone still scoffed. After all anyone can get lucky once. They started paying attention when she got lucky twice. They still laughed a bit with a wary look in their eyes. However, after seeing her naked, covered in blood, and looking down dispassionately over the priest that kidnapped and tortured her, he and everyone else reassessed her. I looked at the bonds that he put her in. Just to get out of them she had to really hurt herself. He didn't mean for her to escape.

"I will try my best. Though I think she's pretty tough. She just bribed one of my personal bodyguards into a private meeting with me after all."

Chapter Three - Allison

The man came back and said very seriously, "He has granted you an audience."

I swallowed past the lump in my throat. He tied a blindfold over my eyes stating that nobody unvetted ever got to go to the inner chambers of Ivory Tower. It just wouldn't do for strangers to know how to get to Renaldo. Of course, I would be screwed royally if I wanted to get out. I did know we took an elevator and we walked a little longer than I liked. He led me into a room with some air. I felt him leave. I reached for the blindfold.

"Leave it for now," a low voice said. I put my hands down.

"Why?"

"Because It amuses me. How old are you girl?"

"Twenty-two, so I am hardly a girl."

"You will be if I want you to be. Besides you are a girl comparison to me."

"Ah yes, I've forgotten. You are terribly old," I said as non-chantley, as I possibly could.

"You shouldn't be here." He snapped. I mentally smiled. His age was a sore spot.

"Well I didn't really get much of a choice in this either," I replied shortly.

"What do you want?"

"You know Cassandra James better than anyone."

"Well I should think that Jared would know her quite a lot better."

"Yes, but she doesn't know I exist, so I can't very well knock on his door and ask him to tell me everything he knows about her, now can I?"

"You don't seem to have a problem doing it to me. Jared is nicer than me. You are a fascinating liar though posing as her sister. You do realize that I have spent years digging into Cassandra's past. Nothing mentions a sister."

"That's because you have no clue at what to look for."

"Are you telling me my men are incompetent?"

"If the shoe fits, though, there is nothing more boring that my father is the filthiest hypocrite in the world."

"So same father, different mothers?"

"Exactly."

"You're telling me that you, a mere girl, was able to find out the one thing I have spent countless resources in trying to obtain?" I could hear him get up and I could feel him. I flinched when he breathed in my ear, "Did you do something naughty to find out?"

I straightened with indignation at that. "Of course not! Could you please either move the hell away from me or let me remove the blindfold?"

He laughed wickedly as he stepped away. "Are you frightened?"

"No," I lied, "I just find it annoying." The truth was that I was frightened.

I got him to laugh again and his laughter sent shivers down my spine.

"Liar. Who is your father?"

"Who is yours?" I challenged.

"I asked first," with amusement in his voice.

"You haven't come even close to figuring out who Cassandra James is."

"Perhaps."

"Perhaps it's worth your while."

"What would you know about that girl?" He said harshly. I touched another nerve and it thrilled and frightened me. It also emboldened me.

"I can feel the lie you know. I can feel it ever so slightly. You have spent hours wondering where she came from because surely, she didn't rise out of the ocean like some mythological creature."

I felt him go still as I could feel the rage in him build. I was prepared when he grabbed me. I pushed back using all the energy I could, and I felt him stumble. I ripped my blindfold off because rules or not I was done playing. His eyes widened a bit.

"Who the fuck are you?"

"Promise to tell me everything about Cassandra James."

"It couldn't be that juicy of a secret."

"Oh, I assure you, it is that good."

"What if I deem it's not?"

"Well you can always try to kill me, I suppose."

His eyes narrowed. "It can't be that good."

"It will topple our father's empire and you really, really want to do that."

"Why would I want to do that?"

"So that m-monsters can sleep in peace knowing he has no more power." I hated myself as I stammered slightly over my own words briefly.

He paced quietly and thought. I held my breath because he was curious but didn't want to believe me.

"To kill me or to tell me everything about Cassandra James? Which is it?" I asked quickly.

"Maybe both," he growled, and I shivered. I hadn't really gotten a look at him but when I did, I shivered. He had black hair and mesmerizing green eyes. His lips were full, and he had a strong jawline. Kissable but I pushed that thought back violently. He was tall and had the build that was kind of cat-like. I cleared my throat because he expected me to tell him something important.

"Very well. I agree," he snapped. Curiosity had definitely gotten the better of him and typical man, he didn't like being bested.

"The illustrious good reverend and hypocrite James Monroe, leader of the Humans Only organization is our father. Cassandra James was born as Alyssa Monroe."

I smiled because I knew I hit home.

Chapter Four - Renaldo

She had the red hair that was Cassandra's. Also, the smug superiority that Cassandra would have when she was very sure and right of something. When I looked at her eyes were the same shape as Cassandra's but unlike Cassandra's brown, her eyes were blue. The resemblance was there. I never was able to find anything out beyond who raised Cassandra. She literally appeared out of nowhere. No birth records at all. The woman who raised her had no record of marriages or even children born. The community that she came out of before she came to my city didn't offer any insight at all. Cassandra and her 'grandmother' were freaks.

That lead to a lot of questions. Yet this girl was telling me the one thing that any vampire king would have killed to have. Monroe was dangerous and had been a pain in our asses since we came out of the shadows. If what she was telling me was true, the fact that he was willing to send a daughter away and blame her so called death on vampires showed that he was even more dangerous than we ever imagined. His power increased from a mere crazy preacher to one of the leading voices of dissent against vampires when his daughter was murdered. Immortal didn't mean we were invincible. It just meant we were very hard to kill.

"I don't believe you," I said as harshly as I could. Correction, I didn't want to believe her but why would she lie? What I did know was that she was telling the truth as far as she knew it to be. Being a crime lord for the number of years I had been makes you know when someone is telling you a load of crap. So, these are the facts that I know them. She had no artifice. If she was lying, then I had better be afraid of her because it's a dangerous person that could successfully lie to me.

She did manage to push me with energy. How the hell was she able to do that? Could Cassandra? What did I really know about Cassandra? Not a hell of a lot. Other than she was able to kill two of my best. She also certainly took care of the priest who abducted her, and she didn't feel an ounce of remorse as she watched him bleed to death before her. She was beautifully savage when she did it. I envied Jared in that moment.

She shrugged. "I suppose you could call him to confirm. Pretend to be someone from Jared's team. Or tell him it's you. He will hate you worse." Aha! That last statement explained everything. She went to the place that would drive her parental unit insane. I believed she was his daughter. But Cassandra's sister...surely not. I shook my head at that until it dawned on me. I made sure my face didn't show. Just Allison would cause a scandal and destroy the man in itself.

"I am going to check and if you are lying you will disappear." I saw a flicker of fear followed by the defiance I often seen in Cassandra's eyes. I pushed the comm button and said, "Rosie could you get the Reverend Monroe on the phone?" I heard the girl bite back a gasp.

"Sure. If he asks who is calling or why what should I tell him?"

"Tell him that I know the truth about Alyssa Monroe."

"You do? I mean sure thing boss."

I watched the girl shift back and forth. Polite would be to offer her a seat but since I didn't know what was really going on, I erred on being a rude bastard. It's probably what she expected anyway.

"Renaldo? What in the hell do you want with me and why bring up my poor dead daughter, Alyssa?" I blinked in surprise. I got him very quickly. I expected some pushing. Then it clicked. He was expecting something not pleasant.

"Well rumor has it good reverend," I put a heavy emphasis on good, "that you have been a very naughty man and I wondered how true it is."

"Why would I ever tell you anything?"

"Because true or not I can bury you with what I have in my office just now. However, some rumors are almost too good to share or be true."

"I find that hard to believe," he spat out.

"I heard that Cassandra James is your daughter Alyssa. Which would be rather unfortunate since Alyssa is supposed to be in a coffin. I also have heard she has a sister by the name of.... I'm sorry I didn't catch your name?" She whispered Allison. "Allison is her name. I heard dead silence and I knew I hit home. Well I'll be damned; the girl has been telling the truth.

"She is there with you, isn't she?"

I laughed. This was the biggest joke the universe had ever played. I didn't get saddled with just one but two of the Reverend Monroe's children and I didn't even know until now. It just made me laugh harder. I finally was able to stop. "Yes."

"Well she made her bed. She can lie in it. She should have gone straight to Cassandra."

"Oh, don't be stupid, Daddy!" she finally spoke up. "Surely you knew I wasn't going to go knock on her door and say, "Surprise I'm your half-sister. Our father couldn't keep his pecker in his pants."

She was at least as entertaining as her sister. That came naturally it seemed.

"Allison Brickwell, you will not be crude."

"Yes, I suppose I should be grateful. Very grateful indeed. Being your bastard, I could have had a much worse fate if you had decided to treat my monstrosity like you did to your legitimate kid. After all, at least you didn't decide to send me off to a psychotic priest to torture me to death."

Well that explained why the priest had her. Allison was the gift that kept on giving. All the pieces fell into place with Cassandra James. I didn't know why the priest had taken her and neither Jared nor her would explain. I shrugged it off because that was normal for her and Jared had always been good about telling me things only as I need to know them. Except of course this one thing.

"What did you do? You run to the first monster you could find that would be the biggest scandal for me if anyone found out our relationship?" I knew what he said was a very bad mistake and if he had seen it, he would have backed a few steps away as well.

She had been yelling and she had been quite flushed. However, she got still. Her face drained a little in color. Her eyes were still flashing so I was pretty sure she wasn't going to pass out on me. In the calmest voice she could muster she delivered her kill shot.

"Monster? If you want a monster look in the fucking mirror. He may be a monster, but he is also still a man, Daddy. But most importantly he's not you. Also, I am the same monster that my sister is. I was lucky that you weren't around enough to observe that I am gifted too."

"Daughter. You are dead to me."

I heard him hang up the phone and said to her, "He's not on the line anymore."

She took a deep shuddering breath and sank to her knees. I thought maybe she was passing out. I crouched down before her. Her head was bowed so I couldn't see her face, but she was shaking. "Allison are you okay?" In situations like this I really needed Jared. He would know what to do. He always knew what to do. Hell, he even has managed to efficiently manage Cassandra James. My relationships with my paranormal investigators thus far have not gone well. My fault because I'm crooked as the day is long. Crime pays very well but it does seem to bother some members of law enforcement.

She shook her head no. Then I heard a huge sniff and I was almost knocked back by the weight of her as she wrapped her arms around me tightly and buried her face into my chest. She was crying. I couldn't even remember the last time I held a woman that was truly crying. It was different than when my mistresses would cry. Usually they used the tears to try to get something. This, I didn't know what I really should do. I couldn't pat her on the head like a dog.

Eventually, I simply held her, and it seemed to be enough. My shirt was going to be utterly ruined. Not that it mattered but it was an observation I couldn't help but make. She solved my dilemma of what to do next by a soft snore and I was astonished. It had to be centuries since I actually held a woman who fell asleep in my arms without any sexual encounter with me.

I picked her up and was astonished at how light she was. I took her to the rooms across my own which were reserved for Jared when he visited. I felt it appropriate since she was the sister of his chosen. All hell was going to break loose when I got back downstairs. I couldn't anticipate how thoroughly. Waiting seething was Selena and the other mistresses. The word has spread like wildfire. The others were only there because they were afraid of Selena who had been nothing but a pain in my ass the moment, I met her. One had to admire how determined she was. She had accomplished more than any of the other mistresses just because she was cunning.

My mistake was that I just underestimated how badly she wanted those rooms. Not that it would have mattered even if I had. I wasn't going to dare make Jared sleep on a lower floor even though I knew he didn't give a shit. Nor would I have dreamed of dishonoring the consultant assigned to me by giving them lesser rooms.

However, Allison was neither one of those so I could see why she was furious. She was dramatic. She cried wildly which unfortunately just irritated me more because I had the recent comparison of true tears in the form of Allison. Selena thought all she had into the demand. Which again, was probably my fault. I did give in to her a bit because it amused me. Then she made a fatal mistake.

"She's a nobody."

"She is everything. She is a connection to Cassandra James." I replied coldly.

"Ah yes the freak who didn't want you." Okay, I admit that stung a tiny bit though surprisingly not as much as I expected it too. However, it was very punishable words.

"Need I remind you yet again that she is no longer just a consultant. She is Jared's chosen."

"Well I am important and so are the girls."

"No Selena. You are my whore and nothing more," I said frostily

She turned a brilliant shade of purple. "If you don't get rid of that girl then I and the other whores will leave. Then you won't have someone pretty on your side to make nice when you need to make nice."

I suddenly was tired. When Jared was here, he had seriously talked to me about just stopping the games. He had seen how incredibly bored I had become, and I admit I was a bit envious of what he had done in Charlotte. I could do well if I chose to go legit. I wasn't surprised when I looked her up and down appraisingly.

"You're dismissed. I will not take ultimatums from you. Perhaps I have given in to you a few times but that was only because I wanted to indulge you in the first place. You will not presume to tell me what to do. Jared was right. It's time to get rid of the silly games I have been playing. You have 24 hours to get out. My staff will make the arrangements."

I looked over at the other mistresses. They were genuinely frightened. By and large they were all good girls too. "That includes you all too. I'll settle an annual pension on each of you like I have all of my others that have retired from me. Selena though…. you're fired."

"But what will I do," she whined.

I smiled because I was a huge film noir fan and was finally presented the perfect opportunity to deliver the best line I had ever heard. "Frankly my dear, I don't give a damn." I walked out leaving my staff to manage the details which I knew they could handle. In truth, Selena would be well cared for. However, it didn't hurt her to think for a few days that she was destitute. I would need to strike a bargain with her and one thing I knew to be true. Selene was for Selene only.

Chapter Five - Allison

When I woke up, I was confused. I fought back the panic of being in a room that I didn't know or remember how I got there. I inhaled deeply. One thing I noticed was lavender though I couldn't figure out the source. I came to see Renaldo and then I had the confrontation with my father. I remembered utterly humiliating myself and I wanted to hide beneath the covers forever.

"Did you know that you snore?" I gasped from surprise. I didn't notice he had been sitting in a chair in a corner of the room. I sat up abruptly!

"I do not!"

"You definitely do."

"What are you doing here?" I asked trying to change the topic.

"Looking at you. Trying to figure out how someone so tiny could cost me a small fortune in less than 24 hours."

He was mad. That must be it. "I don't follow."

"My head mistress decided it was appropriate for you to be thrown out to the streets. She gave me an ultimatum and ended up taking herself and all my other mistresses with her to boot in that ultimatum. I don't do well with being told what I will and will not do."

"Well that sounds more like a personal problem that merely used me as an excuse and not really my fault at all."

Renaldo laughed "You do have a point."

"How many were there?" I couldn't help but ask.

"Nine."

"I would think that you might be grateful. With nine mistresses you will be less tired."

He laughed for a few minutes. "My dear, I don't ever get tired."

I had a comment like that coming. I could feel the blush creep up to my ears which just amused him.

"They were more for social situations and decoration than sex anyway."

"You don't need to explain yourself to me." I said feeling very uncomfortably. I definitely didn't want to know anything about that side of his life. I was painfully aware of his presence. I definitely did not need to even think of - Mister I-Don't-Get-Tired and sex in the same sentence.

"I find myself in a dilemma that I have never experienced before. You want to know everything I know about Cassandra James. I need someone who can appear by my side socially. With a bit of effort, you could do it.

I bit my lip. It was very tempting. Why I couldn't really say. How much would it really cost? What kind of functions? Would that mean I would have to also sleep with him? I definitely needed more information.

"Please explain in more detail what would be required."

"You accompany me and in exchange I tell you everything I can about Cassandra. Naturally, a wardrobe would be necessary for those events. I will buy the appropriate clothes, shoes, and accessories needed for each occasion. Because Cassandra absolutely was a pain about it, you don't have to keep the wardrobe pieces if you don't want to. You will appear on my arm. Some will be quiet and intimate. Some will be red carpet events with cameras." I must have turned as white as I felt because he added. "Your father will see the pictures of you with me." The idea of a photo of me on a known vampire's arm being presented to my father would spoil his dinner. It was childish but it did appeal to me.

I took a deep breath and exhaled slowly. The bastard understood that, and I was quite perturbed, and he knew exactly where to get me. I was probably going to go to hell for it.

"Deal. Though I think you will regret it."

"What makes you say that?"

"I am an average tomato. You are seen on the arm of blondes bomb-shells."

"Or you could be unusual and exotic. Trust me, you are by far many levels above any of the other mistresses"

I shook my head in disbelief.

"Have you heard the blonde jokes? They are the reason those jokes are made."

He winked and walked out. As soon as he left apparently my team of stylists walked in. He assumed I would say yes. I wanted to be outraged but found it difficult to be terribly mad.

Chapter Six – Cassandra

I heard Detective Anderson sigh and said, "It's PMS isn't it?"

I looked up startled and said with indignation, "What?"

"Your mood. You've been a right bitch the last two days. Nobody wants to deal with you today."

I suppose the look of confusion on my face made him elaborate. "You bit my head off twice. Becky in administrative ended up crying. The interns have fled and the ones that can't hide are walking on eggshells. It's PMS?"

"Oh," processing the last days events. I guess he did have a point.

"Sadly, Anderson, it's not PMS. Wrong time of the month."

"Relationship problems then?" He asked hopefully.

I thought about it. "Maybe. He wants me to live at The Endless Night full-time. We've had some significant fights over it."

"Well given that you are there most nights, anyway, is it really that unreasonable of an expectation?"

"Yes! It's very unreasonable."

"Why?"

"I can't really explain it. It's like if I am underground to long my abilities aren't as sharp."

"Cassandra, The Endless Night is 45 stories tall. It's the largest privately-owned building in the world. I'm sure if you ask, he could provide you with a place to live that isn't underground. He could probably even let you have your own stuff so that you're not missing out."

Feeling defensive over the very logical solution that I probably should have thought of myself except that it meant a more public commitment to Jared I changed the subject, "And how is your own efforts going in that front?"

I knew he had asked Melina to move in with him and she had refused.

"You're changing the subject and that isn't fair. Besides Melina's hang up isn't me, personally. It's got everything to do with the fact that I live an hour from The Endless Night. Ours is logistic, not commitment based. Also, she seems to think if we live together it will affect my career."

I wouldn't say it to Anderson, but she had a point. It would affect him. He might not care but it would. There was an insidious movement that has begun where laws have been enacted to see if a now more conservative supreme court will overturn the protections that the monsters have enjoyed. If it weren't for vampires like Jared, who invested so much into real estate and the economic growth of other cities, that if he fell, the US economy and probably the global one would feel its impact most keenly. But that was sometimes not a good enough argument for the religious nut jobs. However, even Renaldo was paying attention because he had hired it appears a PR rep to clean up his image and has been telling Jared he wants to exit the crime world, he's just got to figure out how to do it without getting everyone killed. I personally think that a rat is a rat.

"I know she is right, Cassandra. You don't need to not tell me. Your father called me at home incidentally. Is he okay?"

Oh, my father. Yeah, I've been ignoring his calls. On purpose. I didn't want to talk to him. The Reverend James Monroe most definitely fit the category of religious nut job. Besides, if it was really important, he'd leave a damn message.

"How would I know? I'm not really interested."

"Well he's asking for a meeting."

I looked Anderson directly in the eyes. "Nothing good ever comes from my interactions with that man. The last time I laid eyes on him, I nearly died. Even if you think that meeting him in person would be a good idea, Jared would completely shit over it. And if Jared has a shit fit, do you think Melina won't have a shit fit? She has to deal with him."

"Fair point. However, I am of the belief to keep your friends close and your enemies closer. Especially, after the abduction you won't talk about not even to the therapist."

"Because there's nothing to talk about!" I snapped. "It happened. I survived. I killed him. I was rescued. End of story. I don't feel like talking about it." Because I added to myself silently that I already woke up screaming from the nightmares. I knew from experience that talking would make them worse.

"Renaldo rescued you."

"He didn't exactly have a choice. He has to obey Jared to a point. Especially after Jared made me his Chosen." Being made a Chosen was very disconcerting to me as well. I tried not to think too hard on it. However, what it boiled down to was that it was like an engagement except I wasn't asked. I kind of got dragged along for the ride of it. It was a point that Jared tried not to make too much of a point of it.

"The Chosen bit bothers you too."

"Of course, it does but I don't exactly have a choice about it," I said bitterly.

"I love you like a sister, Cassandra. I have to ask; do you love him?"

I froze. Nobody had asked me that. Did I love him? The fact that yes came immediately told me. "Yeah, I do."

"Then just enjoy it. You're picking at it. He's not going to leave you. There's nothing you can do. Even if you went off and cheated on him, he'll be waiting for you when you got back home."

I hated when Anderson probed me. He had no filters, and because he didn't have those filters he tended to go straight to the heart of things. He literally didn't believe in being delicate. Based on Melina's history, I could see why that appealed to her. She didn't ever have to worry about where she stood. I think my biggest problem was what Anderson said. He's not going to just leave. However, I didn't want to fall into a sense of false security.

My life could really be summed up into two words: It's complicated. The worst part of it was that it was complications of my own making. It was a very bad habit I was going to have to break at some point.

Chapter Seven - Renaldo

I knew the mistresses were hated and loathed by everyone who had to deal with them on a day to day basis. I had no idea the level until the lot were gone and the people who usually deal with them got Allison. It was as if the entire place had breathed a gigantic sigh of relief.

I noticed something was up when Andre who was in charge of making sure everything went well demanded an audience. I sighed and was prepared for the litany of complaints. Instead he walked in and the man was smiling. I didn't know he could smile. "Yes?"

"Boss, I have some complaints."

"What kind of complaints?" I hadn't seen Allison since she arrived three weeks ago.

"She has zero interest in jewelry or makeup. She won't let me use designer labels. She is very price conscious. She demands we tell her how much something costs. When I tell her money is no object, she says send the difference to charities. She just doesn't understand that perfection can be bought."

"Well her father is a preacher." I was trying very hard not to laugh at his expense. He was also unfortunately giving me the seed of a great idea. I added, "I suppose I could send her away," I said adding as much reluctance into my voice as I could.

"Oh no! Don't do that! I just wish she would let me spend just a little more on her. However, with that being said please keep her. I will make her always look spectacular despite herself. She is kind and even though our arguments on her appearance are heated she is just stubborn. She isn't mean."

"The others were?"

I knew that Selene had been difficult. The others too. I had not realized they were mean.

"Forgive me, but yes. Selene being the worst I have ever seen. There is difficult. Then there is cruel."

Yes, I was absolutely sure that Allison was difficult. If for no other reason than when I thought of her conversation with her father.

"She isn't vain or arrogant. She insists we call her Ally."

"What did you have to call the others?"

"Madame."

I snorted. "Figures."

"She insists that we take breaks and has ordered in if we work with her through a perceived meal. She seems to really like pizza and she actually eats. She is very shy and outside of the designer labels. I fear I am going to put her into something that she isn't comfortable in, but she won't say something just to keep me happy."

I was glad I was sitting. Usually Andre was quite shrill when he presented problems to me. I just assumed that was how he was. Apparently, only when faced with a group of demanding prima donnas. After he left, I looked at footage of her interactions with them. She laughed, sparkled, and had my staff eating out of the palm of her hand. It made me wonder if this would be how Cassandra should have been. I was starting to see how the trauma of her life lead her to be what she became.

Allison was different and I was drawn to it. The devil drawn to the angel so to speak. I also wanted to push it as far away as I could so I wouldn't destroy or ruin the angel. Yet…. maybe there was hope for me? I was tired of crime. I had been a criminal since I was a kid in my human life. I had been considering carefully for some time how to exit the criminal underworld without getting a number of people who were innocent killed as part of it. Jared had long been at me to switch and when he was last here, he urged it again. The vampire situation was precarious. We needed to make ourselves indispensable or we would be back in the same spot vampires found ourselves in centuries ago.

No, he had a point and the game had become boring. He made a number of suggestions. A lavish resort and a variety of charitable works were his suggestions. Allison had a background in business and had done a few PR things for her father's church. The idea of making her my PR rep was definitely a good one.

Chapter Eight - Allison

I knew Renaldo was rich. You can't spend a minute in his Ivory Tower and not realize it. I knew I could have anything I wanted too. The problem was that I knew it would be temporary and I definitely didn't want to get used to it. I didn't care that I was repeatedly told by his staff that everyone that accompanies the vampire king got to keep their items. I didn't plan on doing it. It would smack at something dirty and I didn't like that idea.

I couldn't even begin to fathom even wearing some of the items suggested for me. Ultimately, I was expendable. I had been here for several weeks and I hadn't seen Renaldo in that time. As my frustrated mounted because I had not learned anything whatsoever, I started working out. He had the most amazing gym I had ever seen. When I went there it was usually empty.

When I walked into the gym today it wasn't empty. Think of the Devil and he will be sure to show up. Renaldo was in the gym working out and I was in awe. It never occurred to me that vampires would work out. I didn't know why he had the gym. I just assumed it was for his bodyguards or decoration.

He wasn't wearing a shirt and wore a pair of black sweatpants. He was surprisingly muscular but not bodybuilder like. I didn't really notice much the one time I touched him but then I wasn't thinking much of those details. I still blushed in embarrassment over it. Given he picked me up and carried me himself I should have known he was reasonably strong. He was graceful in a cat like manner when he moved. I was in awe of how he moved with lithe grace.

"Did you know that Cassandra killed my two top lieutenants?"

I was surprised because I didn't think he was aware I was here.

"I heard some of the story. My f-father shared some of it when he was confessing. How did she do it?"

"Beats the hell out of me. I was just as surprised as probably them when they found themselves being faced with a true death. I honestly figured the little fool was going to finally get out of my hair."

"Why do you hate her?"

"Actually, I like her well enough. I admire her bravery. I know I scare the hell out of her, but she doesn't give me an inch. That night when she was abducted and of all the cities brought here...if she had died, I would have been profoundly grateful and would have missed her. I miss her a little now. She was truly a worthy adversary. She doesn't realize the full scale of it and even if she did, she wouldn't have given a rats ass, but she had successfully interfered with a deal that had cost me a good amount of time and money working on."

"Was it legal?"

He snorted. "Of course, it wasn't." He said it matter of factly.

I knew he was very much into crime. My father made me perfectly clear on it. I felt rather stupid asking it and closed my eyes as I blushed. I opened my eyes suddenly when I felt a hand cupping my face. I was met with intense green eyes. How did he get to me so fast? I was aware of him.

"Do you have any more questions for me?"

"No," I whispered barely finding my voice.

"Don't lie. I can feel a million questions just waiting for me the second you stepped into the gym."

"You were aware of me from the start?"

"Of course. If I couldn't have heard you open the door, I could smell you, almost taste you on the tip of my tongue. I can hear your heartbeat and feel your blood flow. "He was approaching me like I was his prey and he was stalking it. "I can feel your heartbeat speed up even now." Soon he was right at me. He leaned down and whispered in my ear, "You liked watching me, didn't you?"

I jerked away from him furious because the damn man read me like a fucking open book. "Actually, I was only surprised that vampires worked out." I turned my back and started towards the exit of the gym.

"Oh, that was all?" He said loudly.

"Of course, it was."

"I'll let you have it. I will be joining you for dinner tonight. Your education on Cassandra such as it is will begin."

I nodded and left. I could feel him watching me and my cheek absolutely burned from his touch.

Chapter Nine - Renaldo

It was pure accident that I was at the gym when Allison decided to come to the gym. I knew she was coming to it on a regular basis. Either I misjudged the timing, or she changed her schedule. Either way it was a pure accident and her entire presence filled the gym. I could hear her breaths and heartbeat. If I had been a much younger vampire, I would be compelled to drink from her. Fortunately for her I had several centuries under my belt.

Male birds are ridiculous because they show off to the female counterparts. When I realized I was being a bird I stopped immediately. I was surprised and angry at myself. I was letting this slip of a girl have an effect on me in ways that hadn't happened in centuries. I was constantly reminding myself that she was only twenty-two years old. Though my older and less wise inner self reminded me that in comparison to when I was born, she would have been an old maid.

I could feel a million questions that she wanted to ask me and was furious when she whispered no. Her heart was beating rapidly, and I found myself touching her. Her cheek was warm and smooth under my hand. For a very brief moment I didn't know what I wanted to do: kiss her or drink her blood. Both ideas definitely appealed to me.

The fact that she unconsciously licked her lips out of nervousness had not helping the situation. I knew it was going to annoy her, I even told her that I knew she was enjoying watching me. She saved me from making a potentially bad decision when she jerked away from me. She gave me a look that would have made her sister shout, "Bravo!". Then she got plenty of distance away from me. If her sister was here, she would probably attempt to kill me for the impure thoughts and applaud her sister too.

I silently sighed with relief and I informed her I would be joining her for dinner. I heard Bruce clear his throat which unconsciously reminded me that I was not alone. I groaned inwardly. That was definitely one of those moments I didn't want witnessed by anyone.

"How much did you see?"

"All of it," he said cheerfully.

"I was ridiculous."

"I wouldn't go as far as to saying that, boss. Entertaining would be the word."

"You're not helping yourself."

He flashed me a grin filled with glee. "Dinner for two I would assume. Dining in or out?"

"Book Angelo's. She should get a chance to experience Chicago and I don't believe she has left the Ivory Tower since she arrived."

"I assume cost is no object?"

"You assume correctly. Just get it done."

I didn't like that I was becoming entertainment for everyone who worked for me. It did make me briefly consider if I was entertainment to them when it came to Cassandra herself and I really didn't want to know the answer.

Chapter Ten - Allison

I was furious at first. The man booked an entire restaurant for just us. Myself, him and of the two of us and I was the only one who was going to eat. I didn't like it one single bit. It was high handed. It was wasteful. It was arrogant. I might have some serious disagreements with my father at the moment, but he did not raise me to be like this. Maybe it was going to be inconvenient for Renaldo, but I couldn't help what was just plain common sense to who I am. Then I learned by accident that just down the street was a homeless shelter.

Renaldo, vampire king of Charlotte was going to learn a lesson. One hour later, I had arranged for that private dinner to be graced with the entire homeless shelter down the street. I arranged the press and two hours later I had word that the local news decided to cover it. It was the best win-win that I could come up with. Revenge for him being arrogant, selfish, and high handed. The best publicity an independently owned business would ever get, and Renaldo gets just a tiny bit of redemption but more importantly by being forced to be in the spotlight he was going to hate having to play nice guy.

One of the assistants that got assigned to me was afraid he was going to be angry. I ignored it. I took the attitude that if he was going to be angry that was just too bad for him.

"Of course, he is going to be angry. Then he will realize the press boost and get over it."

She shook her head and did what I asked. Then I got ready for my first event. I knew my first event was going to make my father foam at the mouth. What I wasn't counting on was that nobody bothered to tell Renaldo. He was clearly confused when we pulled up to a media circus.

"You did what?!?" He hissed in my ear as he took in the entire scene.

"I invited the homeless shelter down the road."

"And you didn't think to ask me?"

"Actually no, I didn't. I figured you didn't ask me how I felt about doing something as insanely over the top and wasteful."

"I couldn't ring your neck I suppose?"

"In full view of the media? Not likely at the moment. Besides just think, it will improve your image."

"Do you think my image needs improving?"

"Of course, it does. If you're going to be a criminal, why not be a philanthropic one?"

"A philanthropic criminal? Aren't you afraid this will make me look weak to anyone who might be my enemy?"

"Not really. One good act, I doubt will make a lasting impact. When we step out take a deep breath and think Robin Hood."

"Right. Robin Hood," he said sarcastically as the car door opened for him to step out. I knew he was flabbergasted. I knew I had surprised him like he hadn't been surprised before. Or at least in a very long time. I even felt a little bad about it. Especially when he was forced to kiss babies, pose with mothers, and more or less make nice with people he never intended to make nice too. However, he was brilliant when put in the spotlight. He truly was king of the vampires here in Chicago.

I didn't much like how he would glance at me and I knew he was giving me a look that said I would pay for this later on. Everyone won. Renaldo won because he was about to get for a change good press. The homeless won because the spotlight was shifted onto them and maybe lasting change would occur. The restaurant really won. Not only did they get the PR from the event they got to make a profit from it too. The next morning, a statement from my father was put out that one good act did not make up for being a monster because Satan attempted to disguise himself in appealing ways to Jesus. I smiled. It hit home.

Chapter Eleven – Jared

I loved Cassandra. She was beautiful when she was angry or frustrated. I admired the strength that made her incredibly unique. I was always aware of her. As long as she was here my life was never going to be dull. Given everything I was learning about the Morrigan I even had hopes that maybe I would have her with me a little longer than most. The thought of losing her was a pain to my very core and I badly wanted to keep her safe. I got more than a taste of that when she was abducted.

I kicked myself mentally because I should have allowed her to kill that bastard when she had the opportunity. If she had then she wouldn't have been abducted and tortured again. She says she doesn't blame me. Maybe she doesn't. I blame myself and would do anything to keep even a single hair harmed.

Right now, she just stalked in fuming and slammed a paper down in front of me. "What in the hell is he doing?"

I had spoken with Renaldo already, so I was prepared for the headline of his impromptu philanthropy. He was going on and on about Robin Hood. From what I caught between his hysterical laughter was that he acquired a new mistress who just thoroughly kicked his ass and that he absolutely loved it.

"Turning over a new leaf? Brace yourself, he has hired a PR representative to clean up his image."

"Suure he is cleaning up his image. What's the catch?"

"Does there have to be one? I have been riding him hard in exiting crime. He's agreed to do it."

"That's news to the paranormal expert who has to put up with his shit."

"It's not quite as simple when you have been in as deep as he is to just stop. He's got his own people, ones that are mortal and have families and lives outside of The Ivory Tower that he is responsible for as well."

"Well since he is in the middle of restoring his reputation tell him to be nicer to the paranormal expert. He is on the verge of a nervous breakdown and that won't help if he ups and quits."

I had met the paranormal expert there now. He was a mouse. Literally. He shapeshifted into one. He also had the personality of one. Unfortunately, Renaldo was like a big cat who couldn't resist playing with the mouse.

"I'll tell him to back off a bit. Should I expect you to sleep here tonight or are you going back to your house?" I tried very hard to keep my tone neutral, but I knew I failed when I saw her stiffen her spine and tighten her jaw before relaxing.

I hated that she chose to sleep nights in her own home now. "I think I'll stay here tonight," she said softly. "Jared, I am really trying. I'm just really messed up."

"Have you even tried to work with the therapist you were given?"

"For the hundredth time, I don't need a therapist! I just need time to sort myself out. Please don't make me have this fight with you again. I am so tired of fighting you over it."

"You wake up screaming every single night that you aren't here and there is nothing I can do about! Nothing and I hate it!"

"It's just a phase. I did that before I was abducted a 2nd time. You of all people should know I have had bad dreams before the abduction."

I wanted to argue the point more but knew better. She was willing to stay the night here tonight which was a win for me as far as I was concerned. If I picked at it, she would just get mad and not stay. Besides, who was I to judge? Therapy was a new thing and I didn't believe a cocktail of drugs to control mood would help either.

She cleared her throat and said, "I was thinking about Detective Anderson and Melina. He knows she has to be here because of her job but they would both like to live together. It's suspect that I stay here and am your Chosen. He couldn't remain on the force and do the same. Is there any way you could find a place that would be halfway between here and his work?"

"I couldn't just give them a house. That would be a massive conflict of interest as well." The detective and Melina situation was a sore point too. I was pretty sure Melina was working herself up to flat out quitting if I didn't do something.

"That is true. However, if you saw fit to give Melina a bonus, she could make a nice healthy down payment on a house of her own. Then she could invite anyone she wanted to live with her."

"And what would I say she earned the bonus for?" The idea had merit and I was kicking myself for not thinking of it.

"For putting up with you." She grinned at me mischievously.

I had already started implementing the plan of giving her an assistant that she could train. Her job really was one that would take up three people. I had never had an assistant who had a love interest outside of my domain before.

"If she will take it," I warned.

"Thank you!" She came up to me and threw her arms around me. As she moved to leave, I tightened my grasp and could feel her breath intake just slightly.

"I've got to go to work," she protested.

"But you don't want to."

"I don't but I have to. By the way, do you have any idea what my father is up to these days?"

"Hate-mongering as usual. But nothing out of the ordinary."

"Strange. He's been calling my number a lot lately. Maybe one day when I'm in a better mood I'll answer it."

As she walked out, I had a very strange feeling. The timing was just too coincidental. Her father starts calling her around the same time Renaldo acquires a new mistress and PR representative. Surely Renaldo would not seduce an employee close to the Reverend Monroe. I made a mental note to keep a closer watch on Renaldo. Just in case.

Chapter Twelve - Renaldo

She was going to pay for this. I didn't know how she was going to pay for it, but she was definitely going to pay for it. I admired her though. She essentially appointed herself as my newly hired pubic relationships consultant. I don't think she realized that she just gave herself a job. She had the excuse to be at the Ivory Tower and at my side. She refused to be photographed and when it was time, she made sure I was very busy.

The owners cried in gratitude over what I had done for their business. It was only after I got home that I called Jared to let him know.

"I've been expecting you to call."

"I suppose you heard?" I said with a heavy sigh.

"Naturally. It was well done. In fact, I've heard a lot recently."

I froze because for some absurd reason I didn't want to tell them yet about Allison.

"Which is?"

"I heard that you have hired a public relations person and dismissed your mistresses. At the advice of your new PR. I also heard that she might also be your new mistress"

I was stunned because I hadn't really thought of hiring a PR person until now but if he wanted to assume it, then I was all for it. In fact, it was a way for me to extricate myself out of the criminal world and put a professional barrier between Allison and me. "Actually, it is more because of my new PR. Jealousy got the better of Selena and she took the other girls down with her. Also, my PR person while is a beautiful woman she is not my mistress."

I told Jared almost the entire story about the young woman determined to get help from me and how it led up to the removal of the mistresses. I carefully forgot to mention that her father was the Reverend Monroe and I failed to mention that I knew that Cassandra just happened to be his daughter too. I knew what would happen when Cassandra found out. She would swoop down and rescue her sister from the evil clutches of me, the monster. Given the urges I had earlier in the day I couldn't even say she wouldn't be unjustified.

Allison was waiting in my office when I got there. She figured she was going to be in really big trouble, and she reminded me of an errant child waiting for their punishment. Her heart was beating rapidly but if you didn't have my advantage you wouldn't guess that she was tense.

"I want to ring your neck, but I won't."

"Good. All of tonight was your own damn fault anyway."

I was surprised with the tactic of blaming me for what she clearly ordered. It was definitely a new experience. It was exciting. "How on earth could this be all my fault?"

"You have been trying to treat me like one of your w-whores and I will not have it."

I blinked in surprise at the interpretation and I found it amusing. She had a point but still the way she said it I couldn't stop myself from laughing at her experience.

"Trust me, my dear if I was going to treat you like one of them you would definitely know the difference."

She blushed deeply as she realized the full implication of it.

"You are treating me like them with an exception. You're buying my clothes, you're trying to fit me with fripperies, and I feel like I am being guarded."

"I would think that one exception was a pretty big one. However, I do this for all of my guests if they will let me. Even Cassandra though she fought against it. You didn't come here with very much. You're the normal and not the exception. It actually protects you because there isn't a criminal in this city that is too anxious to mess with what is mine. A fact that your own sister couldn't comprehend but maybe you will be smarter."

"What does my sister have anything to do with it?"

"She refused any marks of favor from me. In fact, her being a pain in the ass and me not killing her was the only thing that kept her alive. The crime bosses figured if I wasn't snuffing her that there was something behind it."

"I'm not her. You seem to do nothing but compare me to her and I am not Cassandra. I am Allison. I am my own person and not liking how something makes me like her. Besides she had a good reason I am sure. If nothing else she probably found you as annoying as I do."

I couldn't help but smile. Whatever can be said about the Reverend Monroe, he fathered captivating daughters who had backbone and very little fear of vampires. Cassandra did have good reasons but that didn't mean I had to like it. I just got tired of telling everyone to leave her alone, and that when I decided she was going to be dead she would be dead.

"The point is moot. Consider everything done as an advance."

"An advance to what?" She said with suspicion in every syllable. In that moment if there had been any doubt of who she was genetically it came out. I had to blink to make sure Cassandra wasn't present.

"You picked your job title tonight. Congratulations. You're my official public relations agent. You are solely responsible for making sure my image becomes impeccable. You see, my dear, as furious as I am with you, I see advantages of it. I have been considering giving up my shadier business ventures and focus on my more legitimate ones."

I was glad that she was sitting down. She went white as a sheet. I could tell her hands were shaking but I wasn't sure if it was fear or anger. Eventually she took a deep breath. "I can't do it. I'd rather be your m-mistress."

I really liked her. She kept me guessing. Most people, I can read and guess what will come out of their mouths. With Allison, it was anyone's guess.

"While I cannot say the idea doesn't sound absolutely delicious to me, my dear, I must ask why you would turn down a nice respectful position for something less so."

"Were you the village idiot? I'm not qualified!"

"You've got a business degree? How aren't you qualified? I've even looked at your resume. You did some good work for your father."

"Nepotism isn't experience." She snapped back.

In all of it, it never once occurred to me whether she could do the job. She completely twisted something private and turned it into a charity event! She had everyone eating out of the palm of her hand. It's a good thing she didn't want me dead because I'm not even sure my bodyguards would stop her. More likely they would open the door, hand her the silver stake, and ask her if it was sharp enough or would it please her for them to sharpen it a little more. Maybe it wasn't quite that bad, but it was definitely not that good either.

"Actually, the village pickpocket."

"What?" She asked with a confused expression.

"I wasn't the village idiot. I was the village thief," I explained.

I watched her carefully as she processed it. "Right. That makes perfect sense. How did you get from pickpocket to crime lord?"

"That is a topic for another day. I don't care about your experience. I do care about results and tonight was proof that you can accomplish it. Money is no object. If you need help delegate."

"There are better qualified people than I. I worked for my father. What was he going to do? Fire me? I wasn't exactly public acknowledgement. In fact, he would have probably given me any promotion I asked for just not revealing who I really was."

"You have an unlimited budget, you have talent, I consider it a done deal."

I saw her bite her lower lip.

"Well what would I choose? What events should I do? What are your legitimate business ventures?"

"Whatever, you bloody well like. If it helps, I seriously doubt you can impact my reputation negatively. I am indifferent to your choices. I do expect that you meet with me for an hour every day to discuss what you have planned for me. I don't mind kissing babes...I mean babies." She snorted with laughter at that.

"It just might be a little wise for me to have actually fed before I get all up close and personal. Jeanette from my Human Resources department will discuss salary. Your salary includes wardrobe, hair, and makeup for events. It will also include room and board if you wish. I would prefer you stay here because my enemies will not like my image changing. I can better protect you here. However, if you wish not to, I'll get you an apartment. As for my legitimate business ventures? There aren't any."

"What if I don't want to do this?"

"Well I would hope that you would say yes on your own. However, the truth of the matter is you don't have a choice. Your presence has been noted. My mistresses will sooner than later make a slip of the tongue. I would prefer to introduce you on my own terms than allow nasty speculation and rumor paint you."

I saw her nod her head curtly and not say anything more. I knew she was furious. Her body was trembling with suppressed fury.

"Think Robin Hood." I said grimly throwing her words at her. I couldn't do anything more about it, so I left. I heard a crash of something breakable when the door closed. Why on earth did women like to throw breakable things? It was a centuries old mystery to me.

Chapter Thirteen - Allison

Just like that he ordered my life around what he wanted. A week ago, I was Allison Brickwell, daughter of the Reverend Monroe. Today I apparently became the employee of the vampire king of Chicago doing a job that I was being massively overpaid to do in which I was proportionally underqualified for. Scared didn't even begin to come close. Seriously, his mistress was a lot more appealing.

I didn't relish failure and I was going to fall flat on my face. Nobody would ever take me seriously again. I had some ideas. I barely slept that night fretting and wrote out a list of all the charities that I knew were real and would be good points. I then researched the issues that plagued the city of Chicago. Not very surprisingly crime and crooked political figures were top of the list.

By lunch a plan was starting to form, and he wasn't going to like it one single bit. His personal secretary came to me and told me that she was under orders to help as much as she could. I handed her the list and saw her startled expression.

"That's very good. Very good indeed."

"How much is he going to like teaching kids to paint?"

Her eyes narrowed a bit. "He will probably hate it." I smiled widely at that.

She realized that she had said too much and blushed. By that evening I had written down several long-range projects and some that would be quick and easy to accomplish. In my notes I had, "Painting with at risk youth" in big letters at the top of the list.

I got a message that we would be meeting in his study for my report at 9. By the time 9 came around I was fretting with nerves again. I knocked on the door with sweaty hands. "Enter," I heard his voice bark.

He was wearing a charcoal grey waistcoat with a red tie. He sat behind his desk with his hands in front of him. When I was seven or eight years old, I had gotten into a fight with Martha Pilkerton. She had called me a bastard and while I didn't realize what it meant; I did recognize it as an insult. I was taken to the principal's office. I felt just like my younger self in that moment.

He flashed me a smile that made me go weak at the knees. "What do you have for me?"

I handed him the papers I was carrying. "Why do you think the charter schools will help?"

"If you can educate the kids then they won't be as prone to the gangs. The same with the afterschool programs. Community activities in safer environments."

"There are programs like that out there. What makes you think yours will work?"

"Most of those other programs are underfunded. They depend on charitable donations or grants. Yours won't have to jump the hoops that the others have to do in order to be viable. Will you eliminate all crime? No but you can still try and appear to be a man of the community."

"You have some points. I will greenlight all of your long-range projects. I will send you my property assets manager tomorrow in order for you to pick out locations."

"Property assets manager?"

"I own a lot of real estate. Some of it in use. Some of it vacant. Let's see if we have places suitable for the projects. If not, I can always buy or build something more, but no point in not seeing what is available."

"Excellent." I got up to walk away.

"Your hour isn't up." I froze.

"But we are done, aren't we?"

"No, we are not done. We have to go over the short-term projects next."

I sank slowly. "I assumed you would greenlight them too."

"Well I do have to ask how painting with underprivileged kids is going to help?"

I really didn't have a good answer for it Other than to purely humiliate him and to ruffle his feathers a bit. I wasn't about to give him the satisfaction of it. "It will make you appear to be a benevolent godfather?"

Chapter Fourteen - Renaldo

I loved watching her squirm. She was too damn cute when put on the spot like that. I was going to have to give her a reprieve but first a little more squirming. I loved the term, "benevolent godfather". It might be a way to bridge the gap between who I am and who I was going to need to be. Plus, it was just too damn funny.

It would give me some options in being able to keep everyone safe. I knew my world. Fear was a powerful thing. It kept people in line. It kept those you wanted to keep safe from danger. Though the real key is never to have anyone close enough. It would leave my cards on the table and if I needed to, I could strike brutally.

I knew she chose the painting with kids to utterly and completely humiliate me. It was a brilliant idea though. I could see how it could fit.

"Exposure to the arts at a young age is linked to higher test scores." She said calmly but judging by the beat of her heart she was anything but calm. I stood up and walked around the desk. "Really?" I drawled. "Really," she said breathlessly. I leaned over and whispered in her ear, "Then why is your heart beating so fast?"

It wasn't just her heart racing. She was slightly flushed. She kept licking her lips in her nervousness and the smell of her hair was just a light fragrance but oh so very perfect for her. I wanted very badly to kiss her, and I knew she wanted me to kiss her as well. But I knew once I did, I'd want to do it again, and again.

She flushed as I walked back around to my desk. Getting that close to her was a very bad idea for me and for her. "I don't care if you are trying to humiliate me. Just admit to the truth of it rather than come up with some other excuse. I said it more harshly than I really intended.

"May I leave now?" She asked angrily.

"Yes." She stormed out slamming the door behind her. I had obviously hit a nerve and damn me, but it was as arousing as it was funny. I was going to have to rethink the not having a mistress approach.

Chapter Fifteen - Allison

I was royally pissed, and I didn't have a good reason to be. He called me out on an excuse that I found after the fact. Something I knew he probably would have. Yes, it was annoying that he found it amusing which made me feel like I was a child that I had just got caught doing something naughty but cute. But I shouldn't have been this pissed.

I flopped on the bed and tried to take several deep breaths to calm myself down. What I really wanted to do was open the door and slam it a few more times. I wondered if Cassandra had the same feelings with her interactions with Renaldo. If she did, she should be up for sainthood.

Why was I so fucking mad? I started to break down the entire interaction to figure out what was the tipping point. It was the point when he got up and when he whispered in my ear. I could almost feel his breath just thinking about it. Perhaps I wouldn't wash my ear for a few days. My spine had shivered, my stomach leaped, and he moved past me. Just brushing me slightly but I had felt it and I wanted more.

Holy shit, I am royally pissed off because he hasn't kissed me. Wow. Did I really want him to kiss me though? My body definitely was saying yes to the idea. My mind said that it was a very, very bad idea and even if it wasn't, I would be the last person in the world he would kiss. Renaldo chose women with unusual beauty. Tall, blonde, all legs, thin, and with pouty mouths and expressions. He wasn't going to pick a girl who spent most of her formative years with the nickname, Carrots.

What the hell was he about? More to the point, what the hell was I about? Why was I suddenly becoming an absolute potty mouth for that matter? In all seriousness, did I really want him to kiss me? Logic said hell no and run to Charlotte as fast as I could. The other part of me said that I should have turned my head the fraction it took the next time he had me pinned. To be brave and throw the cards as they may. I grew up being told that vampires were evil. That vampires were nothing more than blood sucking monsters who deserved to be sent to the fiery pits of hell. Yet, something didn't ring true and I was always curious about the things that went bump in the night.

In the weeks since I met Renaldo, I could see something different. He was a vampire, but he was a man as well. A man who seemed to be wanting to change his image. Did he really want to stop being a crime boss? I knew the answer to that. I knew one thing without question, he was committed to fixing his image.

The question why I couldn't understand. Unable to stop thinking, I changed into my gym clothes. I found over the brief time I had been here that his gym was a source of comfort. I'd never really been into athletics, so it was kind of a surprise to me.

Chapter Sixteen - Renaldo

I heard a knock on my office door and was surprised that Bruno walked in, his entire energy of a man distressed. "You have something to tell me?"

"Were you cruel to Ally tonight?"

"You came to ask me if I was cruel to Allison?" I cringed because everyone was starting to call her Ally. Apparently, that was her chosen name.

"No. However, she's been in the gym for over an hour punching the bags without really the proper gloves. We're starting to get concerned. Her hands are going to hurt like hell in the morning."

I inwardly groaned. My staff really had taken a liking to her.

"I see. I wasn't mean to her. I merely pissed her off. The real reason you came?" I added the last because I had a feeling there was more than outrage over Allison. I watched Bruno shift back and forth a bit.

"Word on the street is that there has been a hit put out on her."

Having lived as long as I had given me a perfect poker face, but I really was raging inside. How dare someone put a hit on someone under my protection. Calmly in an almost bored tone I asked, "Any idea who?"

"Not yet but I speak for all the people here, we'll find out boss. I just thought it might be best you knew in case you wanted to take special precautions."

My mind was racing on who would target her this quickly. I knew that any appearance of cleaning my image up was going to be not good. I had no idea it would come to this that they would target the PR agent responsible for starting to redeem my qualities. It was just one event after all. Little did my enemies really understand is that I'll always be a monster underneath the façade.

"Yes. But don't make it too obvious. I don't want to spook her. Find out who is behind it. Don't kill him. Just find out who it is so I can deal with it personally. It's time to show that while I might want out of the crime world, I will always be able to wipe them out."

"Very good sir."

He walked out and I thought it was time to do a little exercising of my own. I didn't want her to hurt herself too badly. Or at least that's what I told myself. When I got to the gym she was completely drenched with sweat and hitting the bag for all she was worth. A few of the guards were looking on, their faces creased with concern. I nodded to them and they retreated.

"I'm sorry." I watched her spin around to face me. She probably shouldn't have done it because she fainted and went down like a pile of bricks. In a blink I caught her. In another blink the gym was filled with guards. Her hands were bleeding, but I tried not to think about that too much otherwise I would have licked the blood from them. Her eyes fluttered open and she groaned.

There was water being handed to me. "Here drink this," I said as I sat her up and she groaned again. "When was the last time you ate?"

"I'm not sure. Breakfast?"

"Don't you know that if you're going to work out like that you shouldn't do it when you've not eaten in the last 18 or so hours?"

"Apparently I didn't know but I do now."

"Good. I'm taking you upstairs. You need a bath, get your hands tended, and something to eat."

"My hands will be fine. I heal like Cassandra James does."

I hushed her by picking her up. She had no choice but to wrap her arms around me. I had a deep feeling that I was about to embark on a series of bad ideas. "Send some fruit, cheese, and bread to my rooms. Maybe some protein of some sort."

The unfortunate side of being king that didn't get questioned much was that I had people who didn't point it out when I was about to embark upon a very bad idea. On the most part most of my ideas were bloody brilliant.

"You can't take me to your rooms."

"Why not?"

"It's just not done."

"It will be until I know you won't faint again."

She squirmed and I almost dropped her. "Don't squirm."

"Then put me down."

"Just for you to land flat on your back again? No thank you."

"I didn't land flat on my back."

"I know. Because I was there to keep you from doing it. Your welcome by the way."

"Bastard."

"Probably. I certainly didn't know who my father was, and my mother wasn't exactly confessing. As for the other kind, you should have known that before walking through the doors."

"You don't have to act like one."

"But it's so fun."

She stopped talking after that. My mission was to get her to my rooms, sit her on the couch and clean her hands up. The smell of her blood was driving me absolutely insane. My mouth was watering.

It wasn't until I sat her down that I realized that nobody came to my rooms. It was the rule with the mistresses. I came to them, not the other way around. Yet here hear she was. The least likely to be here, sitting on the couch. Her hands folded in her lap. I had retreated to the other side of the room to presumably get clothes to clean her hands, but it was really to get the hell away from her.

Carrying her had been arousing. Smelling her blood nearly had undone me.

"Renaldo?"

I glanced over to her. She held her hands out to me. "You can lick them clean if you want."

"No." I said too quickly and thoroughly horrified. Could she read my mind?

"Why not? You want to and I don't mind. It's just blood."

I couldn't refuse. How could I refuse? She was sitting prettily on my couch with her hands held out before her with her eyes lowered.

"Promise to call for help if I can't stop?"

"I promise," she whispered.

Blood. It was everything for a creature such as me. It wasn't just blood. I've seen people try to describe how it tastes for a vampire. The simple fact is that it is indescribable. It is beyond a metallic taste as I have read one describe. It is sweet but also salty. Both a liquid and a solid. It nourished but also made some of us feel guilty for taking. It was a source of life and death. If you were to close your eyes and imagine the best thing you have ever tasted, you can only get a glimpse at what I get from blood.

It was a precious gift for those willing to offer it up and while she was not offering for me to feed, she was offering me to taste it was still a gift. As such I planned to make the gift count. I dropped to my knees and crawled to her. I knew it was affecting her because I could hear her heart pound as she drew sharp breaths.

I took her right hand gently in my hands and brought it up to my lips. "Thank you for your offering," I whispered. I started out with a long slow lick across her knuckles. Delicious is the only word to compare. She drew her breath deep when I did it. If she liked that she was going to love the next thing I would do as I lapped in between her fingers. I started with her pinky. Her eyes widened with shock when I slid the whole finger in my mouth and slowly sucked it, she moaned. I repeated it with each of the fingers.

Just before I was about to start on the other hand, I heard her whisper clearly, "Kiss me?"

I froze. She was looking at me directly. Kiss her, how I would love to kiss her. I could only imagine how nice it would be to kiss her. I wanted to kiss her very badly. I couldn't though. She was an angel and I was a monster. Plus, I knew I wouldn't stop at a kiss.

"No, Allison. I cannot do that to you."

I saw her face fall and she whispered, "I understand."

Somehow, I got the feeling she didn't. I reached for her, but she said harshly, "No. Do not touch me."

She got up and ran out.

Bruno knocked and entered. "She is safe in her rooms. What did you do to her? She was crying."

I could hear the tone of accusation.

"Nothing."

"Well she was crying pretty badly for nothing."

"She asked me to kiss her."

I watched Bruno's face register surprise.

"Surely you aren't that bad of a kisser, boss."

"I kiss just fine, thank you. I didn't."

Bruno whistled low and began to chuckle.

"Why are you laughing?"

"No offense boss, but for being around for a really long time, you are remarkably dim when it comes to women."

"Oh, and you think you are better?"

"I know I am. I'm about to become a father. It stands to reason that I had to get it right with someone at least once. If a beautiful woman of her caliber tells me to kiss her instead of saying no, I'm going to damn well kiss her for all I'm worth."

"I didn't want to defile her with myself." I grimaced when he howled with laughter for a good five minutes.

After wiping tears from his eyes, he said, "That's a noble sentiment boss but again if a woman wants you to kiss her unless you have a serious objection to her person, just do it. The rest will sort itself out."

"You know you're awfully cheerful and remarkably bold in how you speak to me. Why is that?"

Bruno shrugged. "I am going to go to hell when I die. I figure I've got nothing to lose and what's a few extra years in hell in the grand scheme of things. You need someone to tell you the truth and not walk on eggshells. Plus, it helps that you aren't really my boss."

That took me back. "Who is your boss because I distinctly recall signing your check."

"Jared."

AH. I knew he had spies on me. I had no idea the level. "Does he know about Allison?"

"He knows she exists but not that she seems to be his chosen's sister. Didn't think it was my business to tell him."

"Don't then. Sooner or later he will be told but I would prefer to tell him when I'm ready."

"Fair enough. What do you think I should do about Allison?"

"Kiss her silly…. If she decides to talk to you again."

"She's incredibly young and innocent."

He snorted at that. "She's not that young or innocent. She is making plans for you like a born dictator with the goal to humiliate you utterly. I might not know what she is about, but I do know this, she has a head for what she is doing. There's a reason why your enemies want her dead. If you turn friends to the cops you can bury every crime lord in the city. It doesn't help that Park Walter's warehouse was raided by the cops the other day. They think you might have sold them out."

I shook my head. "I didn't."

"I know. Even the cops get lucky from time to time. They just want someone to blame and right now you and her are it."

I did get it that there were crime bosses who would love to take me down. I would be looking for all of their weaknesses myself. Jared wants me to exit the life, but he doesn't fully understand that I'll never be entirely free. You just do not exit underground crime. At least not without giving everyone a really good idea of why you are the last person they want to follow after. I just couldn't figure out how to do it without a complete bloodbath.

Chapter Seventeen - Allison

Can I just crawl under a rock and die now? Of course, he said no. What the hell was I thinking with the, "Kiss me?" Oh wait, I wasn't thinking! God, I'm such an idiot for actually expecting him to do it. It was just so erotic with him licking the blood from my hand. Then again of course it should be. He was enjoying himself. It was blood and he is a vampire.

I didn't think I could face him again and I was going to make sure I succeeded. If I could avoid his physical presence, I might be able to get the image of him crawling on the floor towards me out of my mind. After what seemed to be hours of crying, I finally fell asleep with a firm plan fixed in my mind.

I sent him an email announcing my intention to avoid him all together. He responded that he respected my decision, but he required my presence at the charity events that I had already planned for him. He was right and I made a mental note not to schedule events that required my presence in the future.

I was surprised Renaldo allowed me to cancel one on one's with him. The press headlines quickly reflected the change in his image. In relation, I noticed security had been increased dramatically but I really didn't question it. I was exhausted from everything else I had to do. So tired that I only dreamed once of him licking my hands.

The event that I had to attend was an art gallery exhibition and fundraiser. All the pieces were made by promising underprivileged youths and the money was going to fund after school art programs that would be free to them. The grand prize winner was going to get a scholarship.

Renaldo sent a note that what I would be wearing would be at the event and that I should be wearing jeans and a jacket, "as we will be travelling a different way." I asked how we were going to travel via e-mail, but he ignored me. We had not seen each other in weeks by this point and it was starting to make me nervous.

I asked the assistant as I was looking in the mirror, "How are we going to be travelling again?" I looked like a gothic biker chick. Don't get me wrong, it looked good but just very strange on me. Not that he would notice. I just about have to be bleeding for him to notice.

"He didn't say. Now just remember, the dress with a hair stylist will be waiting for you when you get there. I'm leaving now so I am there when you arrive."

"Thank you." I was incredibly nervous! I wasn't sure what to do. Do I pretend nothing happened? Or do I address it head on. I knew one thing; I could not forget. There were no books to cover, "What do you do when your employer says no to kissing you after licking blood from your hands." Other than of course the obvious, fire you. Sexual harassment courses so don't prepare you for this.

He was waiting for me by the elevator wearing black leather and damn he looked hot. My heart literally skipped a beat or two and I suddenly felt breathless. We stepped into the elevator alone and I desperately was trying to play it cool. Halfway down Renaldo pulled the emergency stop. "What are you doing?"

"Having a conversation with you. First, I have a question. How long are you planning on giving me the silent treatment?"

"Forever seems like a really good idea."

"I won't accept that. You've avoided me ever since I said no to kissing you."

I sighed because I was such a huge mess. I was about to protest though that he couldn't make me do anything if I didn't want to. He pushed me backwards and had his mouth on mine. Instinctively, I put my arms around him. One of his hands was tangled in my hair, the other was on my behind pressing my body to him. He tasted of something elusive and I wanted more.

As suddenly as it began, he let go and was as far as he could get from me in an elevator. I had heard a groan and realized it had come from me and I blushed furiously. "You didn't have to do that. I get that I am not your type."

"We seem to be having two entirely different conversations and before we leave, we will get them sorted out."

I turned my back to him because it hurt to look at him. "I kissed you, Allison, because I wanted to. In fact, I've not been able to stop thinking about it."

I turned around, "Well you seemed quite clear about it several weeks ago." I knew I was blushing and wished I was dead just to avoid this conversation.

"And if you had stuck around, I would have explained myself. Yet instead you left, refused to see me, and now we are here."

"Fine. Why did you say no?"

"I am a vampire," he said simply.

"Oh my God! You are? Jesus, I didn't realize I've been working these past months for a vampire!" I said sarcastically. "Do you have pointy fangs, and drink blood?"

He was trying to pace in the tiny elevator. His hand raked his hair. "You've made your point," he said shortly.

"Which point? The one where you're being an idiot or the point that I've literally grown up to the daily rhetoric of how bad vampires and monsters are, yet I don't seem to give a shit point?"

"Both," he said in an exasperated tone.

"Good."

"I expect you to report regularly again."

"I'll will take your expectations under consideration."

He growled as he pushed the button to resume.

"Why are wearing clothing worthy of a Mad Maxx film?"

"Very funny that you linked the clothing to that film. We are going by bike."

My heart froze and I pretty much shrieked, "We're What?!?"

"We aren't taking the limo or a car."

"But motorcycles are dangerous." I said helplessly and cringed at how whiney that sounded. Unfortunately, I was thinking through all the statistics and the fact that you fell off a bike in an accident you didn't have nice safety things like seat belts and air bags.

"You're afraid?" He asked surprised.

"Well of course I'm afraid. Any sane mortal would be!"

"Yet millions of people ride them."

"Yes, please note the previous reference of sanity." He laughed at me at that point.

The elevator opened and the garage was filled with the envy of a bike rally. I walked up to presumably his bike and aesthetically it was one very impressive piece of machinery.

"You'll be riding with me," he said startling me. "Also, I'm going to fit you with a harness just in case."

"I really do not like this."

"It will be fine, Allison. I swear it."

"Why must we do this?"

"Security. Some people don't like my image improving and you get the blame. We're sitting ducks in a car."

He said it matter of factly. Almost like this happened every day. I could, however, tell it had to be very serious for him to be concerned. I decided to keep my mouth shut and allowed the harness to be fitted on me without protest. There was no point in making things worse and how bad could it be? Millions of people do ride them after all.

Fifteen minutes later, as I had a death grip on Renaldo. Yes, it could be that bad and that those who ride them are missing something. There were advantages of him being the undead. I couldn't squeeze the breath out of him literally. I'm pretty sure if he was human, I would have killed him.

We didn't lead the group which was the first thing I noticed. We were in the middle in a position that one would not expect of Renaldo and if he had been to the back it might have been obvious. Talking was impossible with the roar of the engines and the wind. I did think I heard him say we were almost there when I heard a popping sound. In front of us one of the bikes began to skid and I could feel like we were about to do the same thing except it felt like I was being lifted off the bike. In that moment I understood how essential the harness was. I would have lost my grip on him and fallen.

The air was whistling past me and my right shoulder burned like I had been pinched cruelly. Even though I knew the harness had me, I still held on for dear life with Renaldo. We were flying. Like really flying. I didn't know he could do it. I saw the world getting smaller down below and we were heading quickly towards the Ivory tower though something was terribly wrong. I could feel it and it was confirmed as we were rapidly losing altitude. We ended up landing roughly on the rooftop of a building. He released the fastening that held us together. When he rolled over his front was soaked in blood from gunshot wounds.

"Dying," he gasped.

"The hell you are," I shouted.

"At least I got to kiss you after all."

I didn't really know how I would know that if he drank my blood it would work. However, from pure logic, that if someone is bleeding to death, if you give them more blood they might not bleed to death. I shoved my wrist to his mouth, "Drink me!" I commanded.

"No, it will hurt you."

"Not as much if you die on me. So stop arguing with me you bastard and fucking drink."

"Potty mouth," he murmured. I turned my head just in time not to see the bite. Yeah, he was right. I couldn't complain about him not trying to warn me. It fucking hurt. It also stung badly because I could feel him sucking the blood. I guess I should have expected it. If it stings when you have a shot because of the fluid going in, it will sting when it's being drawn out too.

I was feeling very lightheaded. "Renaldo, you have to stop." He didn't respond. "Please." Still nothing. I finally said, "Help," as loud as I could. He opened his eyes and let go. I collapsed shivering against his chest. Despite the jacket, I was freezing.

"What the hell are you?" He asked me. I tried to answer that I had no idea, but I just was too faint. He moved his arm to embrace me and I cried out in pain when he touched my shoulder.

"Fuck! You've been shot. Why were you so stupid as to give me blood?"

I was very tired and just wanted to go to sleep. He grabbed my shoulder and I screamed. It was like a hot brand had been pressed into my shoulder.

"Welcome back, darling."

"Don't do that again," I panted. I could feel tears stream down my face.

"Then don't go to sleep or I will do it again. The rats are coming to help."

"Rats?"

He laughed with genuine mirth. "Well correction, rodents and it seems bats too. It's all very Count Dracula."

"I'm so confused."

"No need to be confused. Just remind me to laugh long and hard when this is over at the irony. God your sister is going to flip her lid when she finds out about them."

That was the last thing I heard.

Chapter Eighteen - Renaldo

I was dying. I felt the bullets as they went through my heart. It had to be silver because your average bullet would have hurt like fuck but wouldn't give me a mortal wound. I was fine with the concept of dying. I'd been on this earth more than my share. If only I could make sure Allison was going to be okay.

No, I couldn't die until she was safe. Even dying it disconcerted me that I cared about her too much for my own good. I was such an unworthy bastard though. She would definitely be better off without me roaming the earth. I could already tell that I wasn't going to ever leave her alone. If licking the blood off her hands wasn't enough, kissing her sealed my fate.

Jared was suddenly in my mind and speaking very frantically. Well of course he would be I thought wryly. He was after all my maker. Suddenly he gave me a jolt of strength and furiously was questioning me on the girl who looks a lot like his chosen.

"Because she's her sister."

A deafening, "WHAT?!?" It was very rare that I surprised the hell out of Jared. This was definitely one of those times.

"Her father can't keep it in his pants apparently. She had no idea until he finally told her the truth and sent her packing to Cassandra. The problem is the girl had ideas of her own and came to me instead." Then as cool as he pleased, he picked through my memories as only a maker could and stopped at the glorious moment of me kissing Allison. A kiss that never had felt so good.

He laughed at that one. "Oh. If you don't die from this, Cassandra might kill you for that one."

I almost faded when a wrist was shoved in my face ordering me. Jared interjected my argument. "You might as well just do it. If she is anything at all like Cassandra, you will save her from having to find something sharp and slitting her wrist and dripping the blood in your gapping mouth.

"She wouldn't!" I thought horrified.

"Aye, laddie. She would."

Allison did seem pretty fierce and it would be something I could see out of Cassandra. I followed orders and dear Gods I hadn't drunk so deeply in centuries. She was right though. Her blood was healing a wound that should have been the end of me. The more I drank, the better she tasted. I could feel my flesh knit itself back together and then I started to hear sounds. It started out like a light scrabbling and it got louder until it was deafening. So deafening that it took a shout for, "Help" before I would stop drinking from Allison.

Then there was the sound of something like wings and I must admit I was afraid. Then the voices came. Thousands of them it seemed. What the holy hell was happening? "Calm yourself laddie," Jared interjected. "Just focus on me and the voices will quiet."

"You hear voices in your head? Well that explains a lot."

"Dinna be impudent. Else I will make your figure everything out on your own."

"Fine," I snapped back, "Tell me what the hell is going on here."

"You dear laddie just acquired an animal to call."

Even I was stunned at that. If a vampire is going to get one it typically happens in the first century. Sometimes two. I was well passed it.

"Shouldn't that have already happened?"

"Apparently, you're a late bloomer. Or something about Allison's blood triggered the growth spurt."

"Rats?" I asked stunned when I had my first images flash in my mind.

"You will never see the Nutcracker again without laughing your ass off."

"Smartass."

"No seriously. The rats, mice, squirrels, call the person that can call them The Rat King. You actually seem to have the entire rodent population and just added a new one with bats."

"Well that will explain the flapping."

"Your enemies might want to start running. Your cities rat lord is a doctor. Now pay attention to how things are done."

I saw how Jared was able to bring him up and I was suddenly able to see everything about him including his terror that I could call him now. I tried to soothe his fears at showing how good I do treat my people who are loyal to me. He was skeptical.

Allison was badly wounded, and I was trying to save her. She finally succumbed to unconsciousness.

"Oh no, no, no. You little fool, don't you dare die on me."

That is when my rat lord whom was named John Torres took over briefly whispering a series of instructions. When I heard sirens ahead, he said quickly, "That's the ambulance m-my lord. If you can get her down to the ground level that will get her to the hospital quicker."

"Thank you."

"Don't thank me yet. I will be at the hospital and ready for surgery. Nobody knows what I am there."

"I understand. Your secret is safe with me."

I could feel a level of calm start to settle in among the community which started to feel like it was a global affair.

"It is. Congratulations Renaldo. You are the first rat king in millennia."

"Well I'd gladly go back to what I felt was a quieter less complicated life than to lose her."

"You'll get used to the presence. I was pretty close the break of insanity when I got my cats. But I will admit you'll have a tougher time because there are so damn many."

The paramedics got Allison in the ambulance very quickly. "It seems like everything is under control now. Cassandra and I will be there soon."

I groaned. She was going to kill me.

"I'll try to stop her from killing you."

"Gee Thanks."

"Don't mention it."

Chapter Nineteen - Cassandra

I was woken by Jared shaking me forcefully. When I opened my eyes, I could see that he was in a serious state of worry and the first words out of my mouth were, "What's wrong?"

"It's Renaldo. He nearly had a real death tonight."

I sat up quickly with shock at that. Renaldo dying was an experience I couldn't fathom. I wondered what on earth could have nearly killed him. I wasn't entirely sure I could if I had to.

"How?"

"I am a bit fuzzy on that lassie. He was too busy giving me final instructions."

"Oh, that's right. You made him. He would come to you first. You said nearly."

"It seems that a young woman who likes him decided to save him. She gave him a good amount of blood and it healed him sufficiently."

"That was exceptionally stupid of her," I murmured under my breath. Jared sighed and rolled his eyes. "Well it was," I said defensively. Renaldo was a topic we simply were not going to agree on.

"We need to go Cassandra."

"We meaning me and you or are you using the royal we."

"I mean we as in you need to come with me."

"Excuse me? I'm not a fan of Renaldo. Remember?"

"The girl she was gravely injured but she heals like you."

She heals like me? I'm the oddity for someone who isn't nearly immortal.

"You aren't telling me everything are you?"

"Damn straight, lassie. I know you."

"You'll tell me up in the air?"

"Of course. Once we are well on our way to Chicago."

"Fine. Let's go."

Jared was profoundly relieved which really made me worry. Especially with my father being weird and calling me on a regular basis lately. I had refused his calls because I really had nothing to say to him. Jimmy drove us to the airport. I was busy trying to make reservations for anywhere not the Ivory Tower.

"You ken it's not all that bad at the Ivory Tower."

"I think I would rather stay at the bed bug inn before the Ivory Tower."

"Suit yourself, Lassie. I didn't much care for bed bugs when I was alive, and I still don't even though they don't bite me." I kept my mouth shut because I didn't want to fight. Besides the tension was mounting as we got closer to being on the airplane. I didn't know what he had to say to me but the fact that he was nervous didn't sit well with me.

Once the airplane was up in the air I said, "Ok. Spill. This has been weird. Also does this have anything to do with why my father has been trying to talk to me?"

"It might...." Jared said uneasily.

"What did the bastard do?" Jared took a deep breath and sighed.

"For starters he had an affair."

"What does that have to do with anything?" Then it dawned on me and I was utterly shocked.

"She's your sister, apparently," Jared said quietly.

I didn't know how to feel about it. I was truly stunned. Between Renaldo nearly dying for real and the news of a sister. Then a sick feeling in the pit of my stomach emerged as I realized exactly what her father was. "Did he have her tortured?"

"Seems like he didn't." I felt instant relief with that.

"How the fuck did Renaldo get his claws into her?"

"I don't know everything, but it seems like your father told her about you and sent her packing to Charlotte. I gather that the idea of her showing up on your doorstep unannounced was not very appealing, and she decided to take a detour."

"I can see why she felt that way but why him?"

"Rebellion. From my understanding she had a spectacular confrontation with your father over the phone when he realized she went to the Ivory Tower. I imagine he's been calling you all this time trying to get you to rescue you her"

"Is Renaldo holding her against her will?"

"Not all. He hired her. She has been his PR Specialist for several weeks now."

I recalled the images of Renaldo finger painting. Then it sank fully in and I started laughing hysterically. Jared was frowning with worry, but I didn't care. It was just funny as hell. I finally got myself together, "I'm going to love her," I gasped then I lost my shit again. Everyone was looking at me concerned. "Anyone who can make Renaldo finger paint is amazing."

"I should tell you other bad news."

"There's more?"

"Yes, lass and you won't like the next bit. Renaldo acquired rodents and bats tonight as animals to call."

Shit! My successor was a mouse. "Does he realize my replacement is a mouse?"

"Not yet but he will. He's still getting used to the noise. Fortunately, he is really trying hard to fix his image and this will help him. Part of the problem is that he has been in the crime world so long they don't want to let him leave. Tonight, happened because his enemies didn't want him to leave and blamed Allison."

"In essence the real reason my newfound sister got hurt is because of his shit." I said darkly.

"Actually, the real reason your sister got hurt is your father's fault. He could have brought her to The Endless Night himself. He could have told her the truth for years. He could have even kept his dick to himself."

"Fair enough," I said grudgingly.

"Now you need to promise not to kill him before I tell you this next bit of news."

"It's that bad?"

"From your viewpoint it is."

"I promise not to try to kill him for at least until my sister is well."

"I would prefer longer."

"You're not going to get it."

Jesus it was going to be bad.

"Allison is very close to being Renaldo's chosen."

"You have to have a heart to have a chosen and Renaldo has none," I said flatly. I was in reality worried. What about her? As much as it made me cringe, could she fall in love with him? Would she reciprocate feelings? She would have had a different childhood than me.

"You are thinking too much lassie."

"I am thinking just enough. I am thinking that if Renaldo hurts my sister on purpose, I will kill him. However, I must acknowledge that she and I are different, and she might bring out something softer in him than the paranormal expert who mucked his shit up for him."

"If he hurts your sister, I will take care of him myself."

Well then. I was just going to have to count on that.

Then I snorted with ironic laughter. Jared raised an eyebrow.

"Renaldo the Mouse King. Could I pretty please call him Mickey?"

Chapter Twenty - Allison

I woke up to the annoying beeping sound. I tried to stretch but was unable to move much and my mouth felt like it had been stuffed with cotton. It didn't help that I felt like I had been run over by a truck. As I became more aware, I smelled a faint perfume that seemed familiar, but I couldn't put a name to it. I fought the panic of waking up in a place I didn't know and had no idea how I got there. I went back to my last clear memories and sat up rapidly and groaned in pain. Oh yeah, I was injured. Silly of me to forget that.

The woman who had been sitting in one of those hospital recliners stood up. Even though the lighting was dim, I recognized her of course. She looked a lot like me but just a little older. I groaned because I was trying to avoid embarrassing first meetings with Cassandra James. I ached from head to toe.

"Hello. I gather you recognize who I am?" she said simply.

I licked my lips. "Hi and you're Cassandra James." I croaked.

"Care to hear the breaking news story?"

"Yes," I whispered.

"First have some ice chips. I find they are nice to start with after a major injury. If you start with just drinking water, you might throw up."

I was stunned. This was the Cassandra James. It seemed unreal. She was right though. The ice chips were nice.

"You will be tired for a while. Don't push yourself and eat as much as you can and as much as I really hate to say this but let him help."

"Him?"

"Renaldo?"

Memories of him lying there dying rushed up. "Is he okay?"

She sighed. "Unfortunately, I can change that if you wish."

I remembered that she was reported to not like him very much. "No please don't."

She sighed, "If you insist. Our parental unit has not made an appearance. He of course cannot really acknowledge you and certainly not me. I understand he was due for divorce court today. He's probably regretting living in California."

"She knows about me?"

"Of course, she did. Apparently, she always knew you existed. Did you know California is a 50/50 state? She is going to be quite wealthy."

I felt very guilty. "She must hate me."

"On the contrary. She wants to actually meet you."

"This is not how I expected this to happen."

"I know. I have a feeling you planned on never to meet me."

I blushed furiously because she hit the nail on the head. How do you walk up to someone and say, "Hi, I'm your sister?"

"Now to the news. I will give you the Reader's Digest condensed version. Renaldo fortunately or unfortunately depending on your point of view didn't die. He has acquired most appropriately rodents and bats as his animals to call. My heart goes out to the squirrels. Jared is with him smoothing the power increase out. A lot of shapeshifters, especially in this town, are understandably freaked out. The bullet that hit you shattered your shoulder. Because of the way we heal it made working on you infinitely challenging, but they got you. Under normal circumstances you would have already healed completely."

"Has he been here since I was hurt?"

Cassandra rolled her eyes and made a noise of aggravated disgust. "Every day for as long as I have allowed. He fears I am at this moment teaching you to hate him."

"Do you plan to try to?"

"No. Jared made me promise and I have a feeling you are too far gone to have any hopes at it."

"Why are you being so nice to me? I am a complete stranger to you."

"True we didn't know each other until now. However, you will never be a stranger to me. You're my sister. I thought all the family that really mattered died when Granny died."

I swallowed around the lump in my throat. The door to my room opened and Renaldo stepped in. My heart leapt though I firmly tampered it down. Cassandra's face scrunched up in dislike before she sighed. "Oh alright. You can have your turn. Let her sleep if she drifts off. I've fainted by pushing myself too hard."

"Yes ma'am," he said in a clipped tone and saluted her. Cassandra just rolled her eyes. When the door closed behind her he sighed with relief and visibly relaxed.

"You two really don't like each other," I observed.

"Oh, I like her in that I have a tremendous amount of respect for her. However, she was like an annoying gnat that I couldn't crush so I did everything I could to make the job as miserable as possible. I rather hoped if I made her miserable enough, she would get the hint and leave me alone. I completely underestimated her."

"She took you making her miserable rather personal."

"Well she was quite young when she came here but very capable. A fact that I find reflects on you, her sister."

I could feel the blush creeping up my cheeks and my ears tingled. We sat in silence for a few minutes.

"Thank you, Allison. You saved my life and while it's been a very massive pain in my ass, you also probably flipped the switch that gave me my animals to call."

I didn't know what to really say to that. Your welcome seemed to be underwhelming. The truth is that it was a lot hazy to me and at the end of the day I would have done it again. It didn't seem like a big deal to me.

Desperate to say something I blurted out, "What happened at the gala? You weren't there to buy the art."

"My representative took care of it."

The silence was deafening again. Finally, he cleared his throat, "I have a feeling that we're going to be together for a very long time. Would you like to hear how I became a vampire?"

I was desperate for any topic that wasn't uncomfortable so I said, "That would be nice."

Chapter Twenty-One - Renaldo

I really couldn't believe I was about to tell her my story. I never spoke of it before to anyone. However, it felt right she should know. If nothing else she deserved it after saving my life.

"You will be very shocked to learn that I was a criminal at a young age. I started life as a pickpocket. My mother and sister sold flowers and it didn't bring enough money to keep us fed so I found alternatives. I'm not sure who my father was. I have no memory other than being hungry. This was London, England and in that day if you were poor you were less than filth.

If I had been caught stealing I would either have lost my hand or been killed outright. One day I saw the richest nob I had ever laid my eyes on. There is one thing the have nots can recognize and it's how good one of the haves can have it. He was careless with his purse like he was untouchable and that should have been enough to clue me in.

You could see how heavy it was with coins and he wasn't really paying attention to his surroundings. It was prime pickings. The only problem was the man was a bloody giant. He was taller than everyone. However, big also meant slow so I was pretty confident. The other boys were afraid of him and wouldn't have anything to do with it.

I was afraid too. I would be lying if I said I wasn't. However, I figured I could outrun him and decided to give it a try. It would solve many problems with my family. My mother and sister could stop standing out in the freezing cold and the rain to sell flowers. I kept that in mind when I approached him.

Miraculously it was the easiest purse I had ever lifted. However, as I ran away something made me stop and turn around. He was watching me and looked amused. He knew I had done it and maybe even had allowed it. I ran away almost annoyed.

It wasn't a week when he was back with another purse that looked incredibly heavy. Naturally I thought it a trap. Dreams of getting a nice cottage far from London though would be a reality if I was successful and maybe it was just my imagination. Ultimately, my mother could do nicely, and my sister would have better prospects at a good marriage. I went after it and was successful.

It turned into a mistake. He followed me home. "If you needed it why dinna ye ask instead of just taking it." I was very impudent and shot back, "Because every rich nob would be so grateful to give me their purse? I find I have better luck with my method."

"Fair enough, laddie. The last purse got your mother and sister off the streets. What do you plan for this one?" I was hostile and asked him what it mattered to him. "Curiosity. A common thief would piss the money away. Nor would a common thief rob me either."

"A cottage out of London I thought. It would improve things. Plus, a small dowry for my sister. She'll never marry fancy, but a good honest tradesman would be nice."

"What about yourself?"

"What about me?"

"What are your plans for yourself?"

"I suppose work the land. Take care of the family."

"I really canna see you with a plough"

"That doesn't matter. My mother and sister are my responsibility. I will do anything for them."

"What if your mother remarries?"

"Given what a bastard my father seems to have been by putting us in this situation, I seriously doubt that will happen."

"I have a man who wants to settle down. He would be happy with her. He won't beat her, and he is a talented blacksmith."

"I am not too keen on a stepfather."

"You won't have to be. You will come with me. I travel frequently. I move every five or so years."

I found it all very weird that a rich nob was offering to fix all of my problems. The truth was that I wasn't really keen on the farm life personally, but I'd do whatever it took to ensure survival. "You're not..." I waved my hand vaguely to indicate being interested in boys. It was a huge possibility after all. It wasn't as if I hadn't even been offered for.

He laughed. "I am not in the least interested in boys or even grown men for that matter."

"What's the catch?" Nothing for free was free. There was a catch somewhere along the lines.

"There isn't one laddie. Other than of course keeping my secrets."

"My mother has to agree. Also, I have to meet this man first."

"All very reasonable requests and can be done. Time is of the essence. I am moving next month."

"Why?"

"All in good time. You should learn not to be impatient. First let's meet with my man."

I had never been more hesitant in my life. I wanted badly to run away but I also wanted badly solutions, and this was a solution. I also didn't want to be a coward.

"Bravery is not about being afraid. It is doing what needs to be done despite being afraid. I swear lad, I'm not going to hurt you. I swear I will not enslave your or do anything to you or your family that would cause harm. I ken this is odd."

I took a deep breath, "You could say that again. Let's go."

I followed him to a large house in a very rich neighborhood. From the moment he walked in he was greeted with deference. He immediately began ripping the lace off him. "I hate the latest fashion," he explained.

Waiting in a room that was called the study the man who was being proposed to be my mother's husband waited. Though I didn't understand how he knew to be waiting. When he saw Jared, he bowed. "Master, this is the boy?"

"Yes," Jared said. The man smiled as he assessed me and I him. I noted he had all of his teeth. He also had a good bit of fat which meant he earned a good living. But true to the nature of him being a blacksmith he was also a large man. "My mother is small and thin. Will you beat her?"

"No. If a man can't control his wife without hitting her, he isn't much of a man."

"What about my sister?"

"I will love her as if she is my own."

"And should my mother die from trying to give you a son?"

"I cannot sire children. I am capable of the flesh, but I will never have children of my own. Should she die of something else, your sister will be well cared for. Nor will I remarry."

This was weird. However, he seemed sincere.

"Fine. You can meet my mother. Her name is Sarah and my sister is Beth."

"Any recommendations on how to woo your mother? It is important that she wants this."

I could not believe I was going to suggest to a stranger what to do to get my mother to agree to be his wife. I grasped at the first thought I could. "A bolt of pretty fabric. Maybe some sweets for my sister."

The man glanced at Jared who responded, "You know better than to ask John."

"I know better but I'm still going to do it. Does the boy know?"

"Not yet."

I was abuzz about know what. "Then tell him. The lad has the right to know. Hell, the lad has more than earned the right to know given that he's standing here."

"You have a fair point," he then turned towards me, "John is special. Actually, everyone in my house is special."

"Special how?"

"John can shapeshift into the form of a leopard. It guarantees that he won't get sick and die from anything except old age. He will be able to heal most wounds and he will always be able to provide food to your mother because he is a natural hunter."

I laughed because then I knew it was all a hoax. People can't turn into animals. Jared turned to the man and said quietly, "Show him."

John stripped most of his clothes off and closed his eyes. At first, I didn't notice anything but then I started to see him almost melt into a new shape. I could hear bones shift and break and could then seem to rearrange themselves. It was both very gross and neat to see. It was almost unbelievable, and I should have been frightened. But oddly I wasn't. He padded over to me and butted my hand gently.

I cleared my throat and being cheeky I said, "Well it's a good thing you can't have children. You would never be able to explain to my mother how you gave her a litter of kittens."

I think he might have laughed. I couldn't be sure, but he did roll onto his back. I looked over at Jared. "Why do I have a feeling you don't turn into a cat?"

"That is because I don't. The boys, they ken that I'm not to be trifled with even though they dinna really know. I am vampire, I live and exist off blood though I don't need much, and I have more than enough donors in my cats."

"I won't be donating then?"

"No laddie."

John changed back to a man while we were talking. "He is handling this remarkably well."

"He is a unique lad."

I turned to John, "You might want to keep turning into a leopard to yourself. I'm not sure if my mother could handle the shock."

"I thought I might keep it to myself."

"I do have one question. Why choose me?"

"You're fearless, resourceful, and you can walk in the day."

"So can you."

"I am rare. Most can't do what I do. Also, I can only do so much. Most of my cats are helpful but it would be nice to have a human. When you're ready to settle down I will set you up into the profession of your choice. John chose to be a blacksmith."

"I know what you're thinking, "John said. t's too good to be true. I was much like you when Jared found me. There has to be a catch somewhere. There isn't. Jared gains from his people. We make him stronger and as a result he treats us all very, very well. He is not one to bite the hand that helps him."

It made sense. Ultimately my instincts said to trust it as weird as it was. "Well I guess you should meet my mother."

The cloth and various trinkets plus my blessing and encouragement worked. My mother blossomed and I realized how beautiful she really was. Nor did I realize how much burden she was with care and worry until John started eliminating them.

She wept at me leaving but John was there. "Now, now, he is almost a man. This is a good opportunity and you still have Beth."

Beth loved him instantly. He was Papa before the banns could be read. Jared sent his people ahead. We were going to Paris. We followed my mother and John. Jared wanted to make sure they got settled. My mother was not a fool. She expressed her concerns to me one night. I reassured and she brushed it off as a mother losing her first-born.

Jared and I spent a few years in France. We went to Russia, Spain and Sweden. Eventually we migrated to America. That was the near fatal decision for me. I got sick and was dying. The problem was that I loved my life. I loved everything about it. Except the secrecy. I hated that, but I understood. I wasn't done and I begged Jared to turn me. He kept insisting that I would regret it. That I did not understand the heartache. I was using all of my energy fighting.

Finally, torn he gave up and turned me. I didn't go mad with bloodlust like most new vampires did. All of his cats were prepared just in case. Making a vampire on a ship was usually not a good idea. I hungered but I could manage. I figured out quickly that I could fly. Then my mother died. I realized then exactly what Jared meant. I realized that Beth would die as well and her babies after that. Worse I may see them once or twice before disappearing forever.

The loss was crushing. I fell into a depression and decided to do what nature intended for me in the first place and that was to die. I waited for the sunrise to take me. Jared insisted on going with me. The sun began to rise, and nothing happened. By the time the sun was completely overhead Jared sighed. "I suppose I could drive a stake into your heart."

"Don't bother. I have no heart."

I left that night. I wandered from city to city. Crime followed me like an old friend, and I found that I had the gift of making it very profitable. Intrigue didn't bother me, and I learned from the best. Nobody did intrigue better than the French and Russian courts. I learned that I still had a heart even though I had left Jared. Eventually, I settled here. When we went public, the next day I began building my Ivory Tower.

When I looked up Allison was still awake, and Cassandra was leaning against the door. She didn't look cross, but I figured she would be if I lingered. I got up. I bent down and kissed Allison's cheek, "Rest my dear."

Cassandra followed me out. "You weren't meant to hear that story," I told her.

"I know but nevertheless I am glad I did."

"That poor girl, she deserves way more than the likes of me."

"For once I couldn't agree with you more. However, it looks like I really don't have much say in it anyway. Just know if you hurt her, I'll kill you."

"Fair enough." It was. It was the best I could ask for after all.

Chapter Twenty-Two - Renaldo

I arrive at the Ivory Tower where Jared was waiting for me. "Your chosen is ill," I told him bluntly. He raised an eyebrow. "She all but gave me her blessing to make Allison my chosen."

"Well that is surprising," Jared murmured. "It will make it easier to include Cassandra. Do you love Allison?"

Did I? I couldn't say. What is love? What is that defining moment that you say, "Ah ha, I'm in love." I did know that I would tear the world apart to keep her safe. The idea of never seeing her again would make me feel like I lost something important.

"Perhaps. I've never had a chosen or a great love in my life so I couldn't say."

"You'll figure it out lad. Now this is what will happen. You are going to call everyone who can come to you. Be careful to exclude those who have jobs that would be jeopardized by coming to your call."

"Where are going to do it?"

"I was thinking from the roof of the Ivory Tower."

I liked the idea. It was windy but then when was it not windy here in Chicago? It would give me an idea of how large my call area was which I suspected was quite large. In fact, if the whispers were accurate, I could call every rodent shapeshifter in the world which is unique to any other vampire animal to call. This was a huge power boost. Jared and I had talked about it. A demonstration of how powerful I really was going to be a deterrent. That I could find out anything from anyone in the world would be enough to keep the crime lords from messing with me ever again.

We reached the location, shook hands with the reporters who really didn't understand. It occurred to me that this was the first time any of us deliberately demonstrated what we could do with our animals to call. I release the shield that Jared taught me to build. It was like a cool wind through my mind. There were thousands. I reached out farther than my city and I realized the whispering was true. They were already calling me the rat king because I could control them from one centralized location if I chose to. I almost staggered at the enormity and I immediately shut it down saying I didn't want that kind of power. A lone voice spoke out, "But you don't have a choice."

Just in my city there were hundreds and they were coming.

The lead reporter asked me, "What is the purpose of tonight?"

"To prove to my enemies that they should have left things alone and that I will be able to hunt them down. I was shot only because I had Allison, my PR specialist with me. She is now officially my chosen and just for you to understand how important I hold that dear to me. I have never, ever, ever had a chosen. I am officially done with crime and if anyone wants to take issue with me on it, get on your knees. I have acquired all rodent shapeshifters and bats as my animals to call. They are calling me the rat king. That means I can call shapeshifters from all over the world from my city. You will not be able to hide if you even attempt to hurt me or mine. I will be watching. See down below?"

The streets surrounding The Ivory Tower were filling up with my shapeshifters. I was met with curiosity and fear. Fear because of what I could do but curiosity because I was not what they would have expected. It was humbling really that I was viewed as this horrible monster. Curiosity too because I had picked a chosen. Something they would never have expected out of me.

"Is it true she is the sister of Cassandra James?"

"Yes, it is true."

"Is she gifted?"

Jared spoke up as we agreed to earlier. "We don't know. My chosen just learned about having a sister."

"How did she not know?"

"Her father had an extramarital affair. He did not tell anyone until she was grown. He intended for her to go to Charlotte. She chose to come to Chicago."

"Wow, I bet she was pissed," I heard a reporter mutter. I bet she is quite pissed I thought.

"I have a question," a smaller man with dark hair and a large Adam's apple said as he stepped forward. He wasn't well liked because his counterparts rolled their eyes when he stepped forward. Some even urged for him to just stop with his conspiracy theories. "Is Cassandra James really Alyssa Monroe, the daughter of the Reverend James Monroe?" A pin could have dropped before whispers for him to shut up and to quit being stupid were hissed.

"What makes you think that is possible? Alyssa was buried. There was a huge funeral."

"Yes, there was with a conveniently closed casket. Alyssa supposedly died a few months before a young girl came out of nowhere broken and bloody. I lived in the town and it was in our local news. Everyone was trying to figure out who she was. She looked remarkably like Alyssa. When Cassandra emerged, she looks remarkably like both. The time frame on their ages are also similar."

Chapter Twenty - Jared

I knew sooner or later someone would figure it out. We discussed at length coming out with the truth. She was against it because she didn't want her life as Alyssa to overshadow who she became. Eventually she conceded that if ever asked directly we would answer.

I was fascinated by how they mocked the reporter. He saw how things connected and he had very good instincts. "Anything else?"

"The Reverend seriously injured Cassandra soon after she showed up in Charlotte. No charges were pressed. Why if she was not his daughter? Only a daughter would have refused. Forgive me for saying this, but, as someone who had watched her in the media, she isn't perceived as being very forgiving. It was unusual for her."

Well damn. I never thought of it that way before. Before I could say something, one of the female reporters said, "Please forgive him. He's always been a bit off. He's watched one to many conspiracy theories shows I expect"

"You're sure he is a crackpot then?" I watched her squirm to say it in the most polite way. I could feel my cell phone vibrate from the text message that I was sure was Cassandra. When I glanced it said, "Say yes and let him know he and he alone gets an exclusive with me. What a bitch." I knew my lips twitched slightly at the last comment.

"You get a great deal of pushback over that crazy idea, don't you?"

"Yes," he muttered as he looked down. He was convinced that I was going to tell him he was wrong, and he was never going to live the moment down.

"Then you'll probably feel a certain amount of vindication if it turned out that you were right?"

"Yes." I could see him trying not to get excited. He was wound up tight. His colleagues had quieted down.

"I suspect that if you were right, it would do wonders for your career. Congratulations. You are not wrong and instead of your colleagues telling you how wrong you were and how crazy, they should have been paying attention. You literally got it completely right. Cassandra James is Alyssa Monroe. Allison Brickwell is Cassandra's sister by the same father. That really was Cassandra that was in the news in Miami."

He looked up stunned like Christmas had just come and he discovered that Santa Clause was in fact real. I enjoyed being me from time to time. This was really one of those times. "She exhibited magical abilities young and her father freaked and turned her into the hands of a priest who was going to cast the evil out of her or make her disappear if he couldn't. She escaped and her great grandmother raised her. When she died she came to Chicago. The rest is well documented."

His colleagues looked as if they had swallowed something very nasty. They were pale because they missed the scoop of a lifetime. Really it didn't get much better than this. It just toppled one of the most powerful and influential men in the United States when it came to anti-monster laws. The reporter was visibly relieved because he didn't make an accusation that was unfounded. Elated because he was smart enough to know that he would have job offers for someone like him pouring in by morning.

"Thank you," he breathed fervently. "Why did she never come out? Her father faced an attempted murder charge but the prosecutor couldn't get her cooperation."

That was a good question. I understood her position. If she came out, she feared she would always be Alyssa when she really was Cassandra. The scandal would engulf her career at a time when it was very vulnerable. She had to prove herself in another city to show she isn't a fluke.

"You can ask her yourself. She is giving you exclusivity to the story with an interview with her."

He almost fell to his knees. His hands were visibly shaking. "Wow, I would be honored."

"I feel the Q & A is over unless you have another question?" He struggled to compose himself but after a brief time, "Just one more. This is for Renaldo. If you have complete control of your animals to call, how do we know your recent changes are real and that you're not going to victimize your people?"

"Seriously, you are good. By the way, I hunted for Cassandra's past myself. I couldn't find anything about it. It never even my wildest imagination would have linked it to the Alyssa Monroe death. The only thing we knew about that death was that it was utter bullshit about the vampire attack. I found out only because of Allison. How do you know I am for real? To start with the vampire and animal to call relationship is complex. I can dominate and be cruel. I can make them fear me. However, to keep control it will use a tremendous amount of energy and there are a lot more of them than me. It will weaken me more than it would strengthen me. Plus if Jared didn't kill me, Cassandra would."

Everyone laughed and it was true. I wouldn't like it but I would not tolerate him abusing his animals to call.

"However, I will add," Renaldo continued, "If anything happens to Allison, don't forget who I really am underneath it all. I will use every single resource I have to retaliate in a measure that I personally deem appropriate. It will be messy. It will be ugly. Whomever is behind the attack be very, very afraid."

"He has my support in this," I added. "In fact, I will come personally and there is a large cat population here as well."

We walked away arm in arm as it seemed to be time.

Chapter Twenty-Three – Cassandra James

I stared at the number for a while before I hit dial. My secret was out and that meant his was too. I didn't know how to feel. I was a little numb. I had taken a great deal of pain to hide who I was that now that the world knew it felt like something private was stolen. He picked up on the first ring.

"Is she okay?"

He didn't seem like a bad parent on the surface, but he was terrible to me and in some ways not great to Allison though his not great was more neglect than anything else.

"She is fine. You aren't."

There was dead silence as he processed it.

"What do you mean?"

"I mean the world knows."

"Knows what?" He said loudly and I could hear the first trace of panic in his voice.

"A reporter put it all together and asked if I was Alyssa Monroe."

"Well that is easy. You deny it. You say no you aren't." He said harshly.

"But I didn't say no. Jared confirmed at my request. I'm tired of hiding."

More silence before he finally said, "This is revenge isn't it?"

"No, it isn't. Though I might add that you certainly deserve it and I am more than entitled to it. It was bound to come out. If not now than some other time."

"Bitch!"

"Excuse me? You just called me a bitch? Why not look at yourself. You handed me over to a monster to torture. What's worse, you knew he was a monster. You saw what he was doing to me and what did you do? You fucking turned your back and walked away. Yet you dare to call me a bitch? You fucked another woman, got her pregnant, and kept it a secret until the last possible minute then you try to dump her on my doorstep. But like me she didn't seem to comply with your expectations. As a result, she is now formally the Chosen of Renaldo Corsetti, Vampire King of Chicago and the first Rat King the world has ever seen in centuries. Yet I am a bitch?"

"He didn't!" I could hear the horror in his voice.

"He did. You have been digging this hole for decades. So, don't you dare call me a bitch and call it revenge."

"What the hell happened in Chicago?"

"Allison was shot as you know. What you don't know is that Renaldo nearly died for real. She saved his life. Our blood saved that bastard and made him so strong if his redemption is a hoax, I don't think I will be able to kill him. He can call all rodents and bats now and it is at the end of it your own fucking fault. You have spent years spewing a rhetoric of hatred. You want to know why I could face Renaldo when he was at his most dangerous? Why I could become who I am? Because I've never met a monster that didn't pale in comparison with my very own father. You want to talk about the monsters out there? Start by looking in the fucking mirror."

"I will deny it and call you a delusional liar."

"Mama will refute you. You know she will."

"It is still your word against mine. Divorces get nasty."

"You really aren't bright. I look like Alyssa. A DNA test will prove that I am Mama's natural daughter. She took your hairbrush, toothbrush, and anything else she could think of to get a DNA sample from you. She knew one day I would need to prove that I am your daughter."

"DNA takes time."

"You really think that? Forget I have Jared and his influences. Forget that even though Renaldo and I are at odds, he has his own connections that can get things down. In fact, just concentrate on my own personal resources. I have been consulting in law enforcement since I was eighteen years old. Do you really think that just on my own credentials I couldn't get a rush?"

"You're going to enjoy my ruination, aren't you?" He shouted with a frantic panic in his voice and if he was still as I remembered he was pacing back and forth.

"No actually, I'm not. This is an invasion of my privacy. I kept the secret because I didn't want to be defined by who I was born as. Not because I was trying to protect you. I'm done talking. You have your warning. You can do what you like. This isn't going to go away. It's time for you to pay for your sins, Papa."

I hung up shaking. I whirled around when a hand touched my shoulder and I was face to face with Renaldo. "What do you want?" I said] harshly and winced.

"I heard. I just wanted to tell you I am sorry."

"For what? And how the hell did you get here so fast?"

"If it were not for me your secret would not have come out. As for how I got here so fast, we flew. It's only a few buildings away."

I sighed heavily because it wasn't really his fault. "No, I can't blame you. I'd love to but I can't. It was going to come out eventually and really I am surprised you never figured it out."

If I were truly honest with myself, I could have been better at my initial interactions with Renaldo. I did come to Chicago full of bravado and a desire to prove myself and he was very convenient.

"Where is Jared?" I asked after a moment of silence.

"Making arrangements. They are going to release your sister tomorrow. He is wanting to do it tonight. He fears that one of your father's followers will act out on his own."

I frowned. "She is still pretty weak." I didn't like the idea.

"She's stronger than you think. Besides, I would feel better if she were in private care and weak with a security team that will not fail her than dead in a hospital because security screwed up and let someone into her room that meant to harm her."

"Is she really safer in the Ivory Tower?"

"Most assuredly. She's stolen my staff and made them love her."

I laughed at the idea. "Cassandra, is he really going to deny it?"

"Beats the hell out of me," I said wearily. I was suddenly just very tired of it all and just wanted to go home. "It would be smarter if he didn't. He could renounce himself a penitent sinner. Everyone loves a flawed man confessing and seeking forgiveness. But whether he will do it or not, I cannot say."

Jared walked in and as usual my heart skipped a beat. "Everything is arranged."

I took a deep breath. "What's the plan?"

"The plan is that since the similarities have been remarked on, we're going to use it to our advantage. You're going to put on a hospital gown and be rolled out of the hospital to an awaiting ambulance. Allison will be wearing something like you wear and she will step out and into my waiting Limo. We'll go to The Ivory Tower.

"Who rides in the ambulance with me?"

"I will," Jared said confidently.

"No. You need to be with Allison and Renaldo will ride with me."

Jared raised a surprised eyebrow but didn't say anything except a short nod of acceptance. I decided to be the one to wake Allison and give her the update. She was sleeping peacefully, and I hated to wake her up. I shook her gently, "Wake up," I said softly.

She opened her eyes and blinked them several times to clear the sleep. "Cassandra?"

"I have some news for you. Are you awake enough?"

"Yeah."

"The world knows I am Alyssa Monroe. We're going to need to move you because the hospital is too exposed. Jared fears one of our father's crazy followers will hurt you."

She was silent and nodded. "How does everyone know? Does he know?"

"Yeah. Me and the parental unit spoke," I said tersely.

"You really hate him, don't you?"

"It's complicated and our conversation didn't go well."

"I can imagine," she said.

I turned my back and started stripping so she could put my clothes on. The scars had come back slowly. Plus, I gained a few more. However, by them coming back I had learned to appreciate them. I genuinely missed them and embraced them.

I heard her gasp. "How did that happen?"

I turned around and looked at her. "Our father happened to me. This is why I will never, ever forgive him. He might not have known who he handed me to at first, but he knew what he left me with."

"I don't understand."

"He came to see me. He saw me naked, bleeding, and restrained. Then he turned around and walked away."

"Wow. He told me a little about it but evidently, he missed some very important key points. Do you hate me for not having been treated so abominably?"

"Of course not. I am glad you weren't burdened with the same thing."

A nurse knocked and helped Allison detach from her IV and monitors. Once Allison was dressed in one of my dresses and with a bit of makeup, at a distance she would be able to pass as me. When Jared and Renaldo met up with us, they were both looking very serious.

"What happened?"

"Our suspicions were right," Jared said.

"One of my rats heard a meeting plotting to get Allison," Renaldo explained helpfully.

I swallowed hard. I knew this could happen if I ever came out when it concerned me, but it was still hard to understand how a complete stranger wants you dead for not dying. "Well let's not give them the satisfaction."

The transfer to the limo went smoothly. Jared kissed me passionately before turning and walking away. I had to lay flat on the gurney to make things look real. As soon as I was in the ambulance, I turned on my side. I didn't think I was exposing my backside until Renaldo spoke.

"Since when did Jared start hurting his chosen's?"

"What do you mean?" I asked confused.

"The scars. I saw you naked just a few months ago. Your back didn't look like this." His tone was very harsh, and I realized with shock that he was outraged at the idea of someone hurting me.

I rolled over. "It's complicated but this has always been there. Something metaphysical happened between Jared and I that caused the scars to go away. It was like they had never happened. They started returning, one by one after I got home."

Renaldo was very silent and was looking at me in disbelief. It was going to be an issue between him and Jared, I just knew if I didn't clear it up quickly. "Think Renaldo…. When have you seen my back? Never. Corsetti had a brief glimpse when we were fighting. It threw him off guard briefly and that is how I was able to kill him."

Finally, he said, "Each time I sent you something to wear it was low backed. The only thing that you chose to wear was high-backed dresses. I thought you were just being a prude."

"I know but it was really to hide the scars."

"You should take Allison and get to Charlotte because I am no good to her."

I didn't want to start liking this new Renaldo. I wanted desperately for the old one so that I could hate him in peace.

"You are wrong. You might be her only hope in staying alive. She isn't like me. I grew up learning to hunt and kill monsters. She didn't."

"What are you? You're not entirely human because you and she couldn't do what you do."

I will explain it all eventually with Allison."

"Well please do because the not knowing is maddening and honestly is making me freak out just a bit."

"If you break her heart, I will cut it out with a silver spoon."

He laughed that wicked laugh that I was very familiar with.

"Now that's the Cassandra I know."

When I talked to the rodent shapeshifters after the initial panic ended, they were very hopeful and some even happy to have Renaldo. The doctor treating Allison flat out said they could see into his heart and that it was shockingly good. That the darkness was more a facade than reality. I was counting on it. Even my replacement was feeling hopeful.

Chapter Twenty-Four - Allison

Meeting Jared MacAllistair for the first time was almost overwhelming. He had an almost overwhelming presence and I was badly intimidated. If I had ever questioned my decision to not go to Charlotte, now validated that I made a very wise decision.

"Mi-lady," He said and raised my hand and kissed it. I blushed because I couldn't help it. What woman wouldn't be flattered? Then suddenly his presence wasn't quite as badly felt. I realized then that he had done it deliberately. "You're a bad man." He laughed.

"Forgive me, I was curious if you were as sensitive as Cassandra."

"And am I?" I asked him curiously.

"Aye and likely as gifted."

"What if I don't want to be?"

"Your father is gifted; did he tell you?"

"Yes."

"Then you will know that you can't ignore it entirely. Which makes him the worst bastard in the world. He of all people would know that you couldn't help it."

I thought about it as he scooped me up as if I was a feather before plopping me down on the seat in the limo.

"I can walk you know."

"I know but I still did it. Besides Gods help me if you stubbed your toe in my presence. Cassandra would never leave it alone."

I frowned at it. He was kind of arrogant. Definitely superior. He was right about my father. I didn't really want to admit it. I was struggling to reconcile the man who was clearly evil that he handed his own daughter to a man who brutally tortured her until she could escape and the father that while he wasn't the father of the year and was absent a lot, I thought genuinely loved me. I certainly never wanted for anything.

"I am struggling to reconcile the two sides of my father. I know Cassandra wants me to hate him and she has the right to hate him. I saw the scars. But do I have to? Should I hate him?"

"No, lass. You don't have to hate him. Just to understand. She tried hard to forgive him. However, he isn't very forgivable for what he allowed to happen to her. It broke her ability to really trust. She finds it difficult to trust anyone and that includes me."

"She doesn't trust you?"

"She trusts as far as she can. I do know she is always waiting for the other shoe to drop. Only time and my continued presence will be enough proof for her."

"How bad is it going to get for my father?"

"For a time pretty bad, I'm afraid. It will be a huge scandal that will put the hater community out of sorts for a little bit. However, he is smart and shrewd. If he owns up to it, it will be discussed at length for several weeks. However, the news is like a shiny bauble to a child. The next shiny story will replace it and eventually he will rebuild."

"Are you sure?"

"Yes, I am certain because I've seen my share of scandals. Sometimes the center of them. Now whether he gets to stay head of his own church is another question. The Society of Humans Only is vast and over the decades he is bound to have rivals who were desperately waiting for his position to become vacant. Now he will have to condemn not just Cassandra but you as well. All of this based on if nobody finds he is gifted. If that happens, he will never recover from being the world's biggest hypocrite."

"At least you're honest."

"I can only predict based on what I have seen in history and history tends to be very repetitive."

I was very tired, and I was going to be glad to have my own bed. Cassandra was right about the exhaustion. In fact, I found myself being caught leaning closer to Jared. I kept struggling because I didn't want Renaldo to think that I was making a play for Jared.

"Shhh. He is going to be fine if you lay your head down on me. He wants you to get well."

The words were strangely soothing and with that I gave up the struggle and closed my eyes.

Chapter Twenty-Five - Renaldo

I'm a fairly observant man. You can't survive in the vampire world or the criminal world by keeping your eyes closed. How could I ever have missed Cassandra being horribly scarred? It began between her shoulder blades and went down to presumably her behind. Would it have changed anything if I had known? Probably not, I snorted to myself. In fact, it would have been something I might have used against her. Looking back, I realized I had seen glimpses of a scar here and there. Only when she was fighting were there glimpses that I dismissed as tricks of lighting. And if I saw a scar or two? I would have assumed that anyone in her line of work is bound to have some injuries along the way.

I was horrified that something like that could have happened to Allison and I did wonder what she did suffer from. Cassandra seemed to read my thoughts and said, "She isn't damaged. Our parental unit was a fairly absentee father but that didn't seem to have bothered her that much."

I nodded curtly and we rode in silence with Jared sending silent updates to me about Allison. Apparently, the concerns of what was proper was genetic because Allison felt real concern about falling asleep in Jared's arms. I guess when you put it like that it does kind of sound bad at face value. Personally, I was starting to think that having had the reverend as a sphere of influence ingrained it into them.

"She fell asleep," I said abruptly to break the silence.

"Allison? I am not surprised. She will sleep a lot and will need to eat well for a while."

I frowned because if she was never completely fine after this it would be all my fault. "She will be alright eventually?"

"Of course. Providing she doesn't push her limits repeatedly. We can heal rapidly, but I think even you must realize that if you keep hurting us enough, we will eventually break. Don't wait on her hand and foot. It will likely drive her nuts if you do."

I snorted at that. "As if she will let me. She is remarkably independent."

"You gave her my rooms?" Cassandra inquired casually. I took a deep breath as I wasn't sure she would take what I was going to say well.

"I did but am moving her into my quarters." I could see Cassandra take that breath that lead to her to spat out, "You can't do it. I forbid it."

"You forbid it? I wasn't aware you were even asked for permission.

"She's my sister."

"She is my chosen."

She snorted derisively and was about to say something.

I raised my hand to stop her. "You had better stay out of this because you know nothing of what you're going to inject yourself into."

"What do you mean by that?"

"I mean that you are the chosen of a vampire king but you force him to run around in circles for you and while he is patient, kind, and will give you whatever you need, you're exhausting and make him look bad. Before you start interfering into my relationship such as it is with Allison, you better take a long hard look at your own."

I was furious and I know she was too. I also knew that I hit home and gave her unwelcome truths that should have been given to her, but nobody had before.

"She was your chosen only because she nearly died because of your shit."

I had to give Cassandra credit. She knew how to fight back but I was better at it. At least in this because I had some truth. "She was probably my chosen the day she chose to come to me and not to you. She picked me first and even if it can be argued that she didn't know what she was doing, she chose me when she gave me her blood to save my worthless life."

I saw Cassandra flush because she knew that everyone had to know that she had been anything but resistance to The Endless Night as a full-time residence. As if being abducted didn't highlight the danger to her, she continued to spend nights at her own home. We all knew how frustrated Jared was with it even as he suffered patiently because he knew forcing it would be a challenge. I hoped fervently that Allison would not be quite as resistant to the things that would protect her. I knew me. I wasn't nearly as patient as Jared.

Cassandra stayed quiet the rest of the way to The Ivory Tower. When we arrived the flurry of activity delayed the inevitable explosion. However, once Cassandra saw Jared waiting with a sleeping Allison in his arms she said, "He says he is going to move her into his rooms."

I watched Jared carefully to see what he would do. He raised a brow as he glanced between the three of us.

"I am not surprised that the lad would arrange that. She is his chosen after all." I winced when he called me lad.

"Why? He has no right."

"Actually, yes he does because Allison has not in any way reacted negatively as being a Chosen. It is done and this is how it is done. Yes, you have your own place because I have allowed it. Our arrangement is...", he paused to take a breath and to choose the right word, "unusual. A fact that you well ken I loathe." I watched Cassandra turn red but from anger or embarrassment I did not know. "However, I have never had a chosen that was as badly abused as you have been. I allow it despite having had a chosen leave and before I could save her from the mob she was burned at the stake for witchcraft. However, I acknowledge that is also not you. I know you need time and against my better self I give it. However, I will not interfere with Renaldo and Allison. Whatever arrangement they come to is theirs.

I saw a variety of emotions cross over Cassandra's face. Fear, love, and something else. She was utterly conflicted as she shifted back and forth uncertainly.

"What if he overrides what she wants?"

At this point Allison spoke. "But what if I want it?" she asked softly.

Chapter Twenty-Six – Cassandra

It took nearly an hour to get everything situated with Allison and Renaldo. By the time it was done I was exhausted physically and emotionally. Jared shut the door quietly to our suite and locked it. The sound of the click of the door locking made me relax instantly. I found that ever since I was taken, when I was alone with Jared I would relax instantly. I walked over to him and rested my head on his chest and closed my eyes. "Hold me, Jared," I whispered. I felt his welcoming response and sighed.

I was still trying to adjust to getting used to having someone there for me that always responded to me with warmth and affection. It was definitely something new in my experience. Also, the quiet silence of just being was nice with him too. I was also getting used to admitting to myself that I needed to be touched and held. That it was not the weakness that I once thought it to be. Jared caressed my face gently and I loved it and I loved my oversized vampire warrior.

"I am proud of you lass."

I snorted, "For what?"

"You didn't try to kill Renaldo."

"That's because you took all my sharp, pointy silver objects away from me."

"You're a resourceful woman. I'm pretty sure you could have gotten around it."

"True. It's actually weird. I just don't feel the rancor as badly as I used to."

"It's because despite all the contentious history between the two of you, he came to rescue you."

"I didn't need saving and you made him. He couldn't have really defied you."

"Actually, he could have but I didn't even have to ask. He volunteered before I could. He went above and beyond to find you. He showed up with a small army with him. Deep inside you recognize his attempt to be hero. A hero to someone that he respected but didn't really have any affection for. After all he did make sure that I promised to get you out of his city as soon as possible."

"Well don't expect us to be bosom buddies. He made my sister his bloody chosen," I said grumpily.

Jared laughed which made me glare even harder. I remembered something though. "I didn't know about you having a chosen burned at the stake."

"It's why I have struggled to let you keep your place. Especially after you had been abducted from it. It's my responsibility to keep you safe even if that's not all that modern of a sentiment."

"I know and I do appreciate it. Being underground messes with me and I do have a job."

"We'll figure it out, Cassandra. Stop worrying too much about it. We've figured out Detective Anderson and Melina. We'll figure this out as well."

But I wouldn't because even though he told me not to worry, I felt somehow inadequate because I wasn't able to give him everything he wanted.

Chapter Twenty-Seven – Allison

I woke up slowly. I wasn't sure where I was, and it took me awhile to start processing things. I started with my body. I still ached in places that I didn't know I had. However, it wasn't the pain that it had been, so I was getting better. It was completely dark, but my eyes were starting to adjust to it. When I inhaled deeply, I smelled the spicy cologne that was usually trailing Renaldo.

I licked my lips before I called out, "Hello?" I winced because my voice was hoarse and not very loud.

"Hello," Renaldo said. I nearly jumped because he was right next to me. A bright light blinded me, and I had to blink rapidly to adjust to the light. I gasped twice. Once when I realized that the reason, I smelled Renaldo was because he was lying next to me in the bed with just a pair of jeans on. The second gasp was because of the beauty of the room.

"Wow," I whispered. The walls were beautiful with a variety of colored rectangular stone ranging from shades or oranges to grays. "Where am I?"

"The Ivory Tower. This is part of my private suite."

My mouth went dry. "I'm in your bedroom?"

"No. You are in your new bedroom if you want."

I shook my head trying to put it all together. I gave up. "I don't understand. I must be missing something."

"You are my chosen."

I could feel the blush creep up to my ears. I also felt guilty because I kind of forced him into declaring me a chosen. Not deliberately but still... it made me uncomfortable.

"I am sorry to have caused you so much trouble," I blurted out. "You don't have to do something as drastic as naming me your chosen. In fact, I'll leave with Jared and Cassandra for Charlotte so that I am out of your hair."

There was a deafening sound of silence and I struggled to not fill the voice with babble. Finally, he spoke quietly.

"I wouldn't like that at all."

I struggled to respond because that wasn't what I expected to hear. Fortunately, he spoke again. "Why do you think I have declared you publicly as my chosen if I didn't want to? I never do anything I don't want to really do. Did Jared make the suggestion that I make you my official chosen? Of course, he did, but then Jared has been trying to get me to declare a chosen for centuries. I just tune him out."

"But you're not interested in me that way!" I blurted out and blushed furiously.

"Ah... that way. You mean sexually attracted to you? Of course, I am attracted to you in that way."

"What utter bullshit, Renaldo. You only kissed me to get me on that damn bike."

I watched him sigh and rake his hand through his hair. Validation that I was right.

"I will not deny that you getting on 'that damn bike' was a great perk but I wanted to kiss you the second you walked into my bloody office months ago."

"Well you don't love me and aren't you supposed to love your chosen?" I knew it sounded ridiculous when I blurted it out but whatever.

"I would really like for you stop putting things that aren't entirely accurate onto me. You assume I don't love you. Maybe I do. Did you ever think of that? What is love anyway? To me love is a novelty. A luxury that could not be afforded for. Do I love you? I cannot say for sure, what I do know though is that I feel something for you. A tenderness and fear of losing which I felt keenly when I watched you lay in that hospital bed as your body fought to save you. Now if you want to leave you can. I won't stop you because I am a monster but don't walk out because you think I don't care or that I don't want you in my bed."

Another deafening silence and I wasn't sure what to say except utter my own insecurities for a man or vampire like Renaldo. "I'm not your type!"

"My type? You mean tall, so skinny you can see ribs, blonde, vain, lazy, and deplorably stupid? Not to mention cruel and thoughtless to those around them? No, you aren't like them at all. It is why you are my chosen and none of them ever came a universe close to it. It is why I have never, ever had a chosen. You compare yourself to them, but they do not make burn and you my dear make me burn."

I heard a loud knock on the door followed by the voice of Jared, "If yer not decent laddie you better be. Cassandra is about to come in."

True to his word the door swung open and Cassandra entered followed by Jared and a rather frazzled Bruno. I wanted to die from embarrassment when Cassandra said, "What is the difference between her having her own room and bed if you are going to be here with her anyway, Renaldo?"

"You didn't say I couldn't stay with her."

She pursed her lips at that before turning to me, "You need to eat. Especially now that I know he can't be reliable about keeping his hands to himself."

"But nothing happened," I said hastily blushing as I thought about his words on how he burned for me.

She didn't say anything, but the look said she didn't believe a word. Wisely I allowed her to embrace her bossy big sisterness and did as I was told which was to eat. Which was a lot. I found that I was exceptionally hungry.

I tried to apologize but Renaldo had to say something. "No worries. I don't like to count ribs. A little meat on the bones is always good."

I blushed even more which caused Cassandra to arch an eyebrow. Jared on the other hand started laughing but turned it into a cough quickly enough.

"I heard from our parental unit," Cassandra said.

"What did he want?"

"The usual. He yelled and berated me because somehow all of this is my fault. After he was done being an ass, he wanted to let us know that he is going on TV for a press conference."

"What do you think he is going to say?"

"Who knows. He didn't tell me."

I frowned. The world knew about me and Cassandra now. "Why do you think he treated me differently?"

"Honestly, I don't know. Maybe he truly regretted the past. Maybe because he didn't live with you and saw the things that make you and I unique daily he could forget about it with you. I do know this; I will know where his position is when he is done talking."

"When will it be?"

Cassandra looked at her watch. "In an hour. I thought you might like to be awake for it."

She was right I did.

Chapter Twenty-Eight – Jared

As a leader of a large vampire and shapeshifting community, I was as concerned about what the Reverend James Monroe had to say as my chosen and her sister. I didn't like the man and really didn't trust him because I couldn't predict him. He blamed Cassandra for everything, but she didn't take him doing it.

When he came on screen, he had aged considerably which was a shock. Both Allison and Cassandra gasped at his appearance.

"This will be as brief as possible, but some things need to be addressed. When my mother was sixteen, she found out she was pregnant with me. She ran away from home and made a living selling spells and reading fortunes. She got hooked on drugs and ended up killing herself. I was raised by her mother...my grandmother. Her maiden name was James and thus Cassandra James is my natural daughter born to me and my wife, Alyssa Monroe.

My family is gifted to the extreme. Those gifts are particularly strong on the female line. However, I cannot lie, I have them to a lesser extent. It is how I have been able to hide what I am from the world while condemning those like me. Like I condemned my own daughter. I truly believe it is a curse spawned by Lucifer himself. When Alyssa showed signs that she had abilities beyond anything I had ever seen I arranged to have the demons exorcised from her.

She will tell you that I saw her once during that time. I realized it was not going to work and I did in fact leave her for dead. My wife knew nothing but the story I gave. The disappearance was real for her. She never looked inside the closed casket. My entire ministry has been built on opposing the monsters, but I am one of them.

Alyssa did escape and calls were made to my grandmother who raised Alyssa. Names were changed, secrets kept. Almost nobody knew the truth. Only I knew for sure that the grave was an empty one. Effective immediately I am stepping down as chairman of my ministry. All of my affairs are in order. I knew one day this would happen though I had hoped in vain it would not. As for Allison, she is also my daughter and just as gifted as Alyssa... I mean Cassandra. She bears acknowledgement because she did not deserve me or this. I am for what it is worth so very sorry."

He quickly reached into his breast pocket and pulled out a small pistol causing screams around him. The camera skewed with a man shouting, "James! Don't!" Then the sound of a shot fired followed by, "Oh My God!" Then the camera turned dark.

Cassandra and Allison were sitting there in stunned shock. Finally, Cassandra looked over at me. "Do you think he...." But she couldn't finish the sentence. I wanted to tell her no. That I didn't think so, but I was certain that he had committed suicide. He had the look in his eye of a man ready to jump off the edge.

"Yes, lass. I think he may have."

She put her face in her hands and fell to her knees sobbing. It surprised me given how contentious I knew her relationship with him was. But as surprised as I was nothing compared to the shock from Renaldo. Allison buried her face into Renaldo's chest and her shoulders were shaking from her silent sobs.

I picked Cassandra up and held her cradled into my chest and we just waited. It was more than an hour when Cassandra's cell phone began to ring. She answered it and put it on speaker.

"I'm officer Watkins. I'm not sure if you are aware but during a press conference with the Reverend Monroe a firearm discharged."

"You mean he took a pistol out and shot himself." She clarified.

"You were watching?" He said almost relieved.

"I saw."

"I'm sorry to inform you that he died on the scene."

"I figured as much. Have you called my mother?"

"She is unaware at this time. It's why his death has not been announced."

"As soon as you reach her go ahead and release it."

"Are you sure ma'am?"

"I am."

I looked over at Renaldo with Allison. "Go on lad, take care of Allison," Jared told him.

I picked Cassandra up and she wrapped her arms around me. "We are going back to our rooms. Nothing more than can be done this evening."

As we neared our rooms, she whispered, "I want to go home. Please, can we just not leave?"

"Not yet lass. Soon though, I promise."

I had to make sure that Renaldo knew about the Morrigan and what he had on his hands. Also, he needed to finish adjusting to his sudden power amp. He was doing an admirable job, but it didn't mean I wanted to be careful. As soon as our door closed, Cassandra started to remove her clothes. I found it very surprising how much she embraced nudity after she decided to be with me. "I want a bath," she added almost apologetically.

One thing I learned quickly was not to argue or say anything at all when she or any woman for that matter decided to get naked. It usually ended up to my advantage. I heard the water stop and start but she hadn't gotten in. I stepped into the bathroom to check on her to find her on her knees before the tub.

"Jared, I have a question for you."

"Of course. You can ask me anything you want, lass. You should know that."

"Do you love me?"

I was not expecting that. I did of course. Unlike Renaldo, I recognized it. How could I not love such a brave beautiful woman like her? However, I never said it because I didn't want to make her panic and run.

"I love you, Cassandra James. How could I not love someone so infinitely loveable?"

"P-promise you won't leave me?"

"I will never abandon you by choice."

She was quiet for the longest time. "I love you too Jared." I knew the admission was a tough one for her, but my soul did do a brief dance of joy.

"Your water is going to get cold."

"Will you join me?"

Proof that when a woman starts to get naked just let her. We floated in the warm water for the longer time, periodically she would add more hot water to it the bath. "Have you sold the top floor of The Endless Night yet?"

"Not yet. Why do you ask?" I was burning with curiosity. As my chosen if anything were to happen to me, she got it all, but she didn't like that. She wanted to know nothing about my business ventures or the business aspect of The Endless Night.

"I want at least one of the suites though for security probably the whole floor."

Not what I expected to hear. "Done. It's yours."

"How soon do you think it will be before I can move in?"

"I'm not sure but I can make arrangements from here to start the necessary work."

"Do that. I want to move in permanently, but I'll never be able to do it with being underground. However, if I can be at the top with access to the rooftop gardens, I think that is the answer."

"You don't have to move in with me, Cassandra."

"I know. However, it is what I want. Also, I suppose you should give me the object"

My mind went into a wild speculation of what it was. Another lesson is not to automatically assume the baser nature is what the woman is implying.

"Object?"

"The ring of the chosen. The clunky blingy thing that you've not been able to approach me with."

"How do you know about that?"

"Paul."

Of course, Paul. He would tell her. For someone who was so quiet he was awfully chatty with Cassandra.

"I don't have it with me. I was actually trying to make it more in line with what you would wear."

She flipped over facing me and kissed me. "Is it wrong to want you and still feel this profound grief that I cannot explain?"

"No lass, it isn't."

"It's weird, Jared. I always thought I would feel relief when he exited this world but instead, I feel sad and a little guilty because he would still be alive if I had not allowed you to confirm my identity."

"No, Cassandra, you will not feel guilty over that. You did not make him commit suicide. He could have dealt with the fallout.

He could have handled the months of talk and rebuilt. Instead he chose the cowardly way out."

Chapter Twenty-Nine – Cassandra

I understood what Jared said. He chose the coward's way out of a very bad situation. However, that did not change that I felt some measure of responsibility in tipping that scale. I didn't bother to contradict him, and I am sure he knew that I was just not bothering to argue.

"Cassandra, are you sure about moving into The Endless Night? I'd rather wait until you are fully ready than for you to rush and flee."

Was I sure? Yes, I was sure. Was I ready? Hell no but then if left to my own devices I'd never be. At the end of the day, I loved Jared MacAllistair and he was worth me gambling my heart.

"I am sure. You are worth it. Will it be easy? No, it won't be. However, we will make it work."

I reached to touch him, but he grabbed my hand and kissed me fiercely. After what had happened in the tub months ago, he was reluctant to do anything in the tub with me.

"You're being ridiculous about the tub," I said breathlessly.

"Maybe…. but I willna take the risk just in case."

He caressed my back tracing the scars as he kissed me softly. "Ready to get out?" He asked huskily. My heart was beating wildly. "Yes," I whispered.

Chapter Thirty – Allison

When I heard the shot, I knew immediately that he was gone, and I was hit with a wave of grief that was profound. Renaldo picked me up and carried me out of the room as I sobbed into his shoulder soaking his shirt completely.

He took me into another beautifully designed room that smelled of sandalwood. "Where are we?"

"My bedroom."

"I shouldn't be here."

He got up off the bed and began unbuttoning his shirt ignoring my protests.

"Why are you doing that?" I was trying to make my tone as angry as possible but without very much success.

"Because darling, a certain female soaked my shirt and it is uncomfortable."

I could feel me blushing. "Well it's bothering me."

"Then close your eyes," as he shrugged the shirt off, "but something tells me you like watching." He reached for the button of his pants and I shut my eyes. He laughed and it sent shivers down my spine.

I squeaked in surprise when he touched my hand. My eyes flew open and I was treated with him up close and personal. "Don't you want to touch me?"

I tried to protest but nothing would come out and I did want to touch him. He took my hand and brought it to his chest. I let my hand fall slowly down his chest. He took an audible deep breath. "Do that again?" He says softly.

Emboldened, I did it again. He closed his eyes in what seemed to be enjoyment. He opened them slowly and his mouth curled into a smile. "My turn."

Before I could say anything about it, he was kissing me. He had his hands in my hair, completely putting me in his control. It was a slow and deliberate kiss. As if he had hours just to do this one thing. Then I realized that he did. I was in deep trouble. He stopped, "Stop thinking, darling."

"I can't help it. I can't possibly be a good match for you."

"He grabbed my hand and pressed it against the obvious bulge of his pants. I jerked my hand back blushing. "Did you feel that? Only you, my dear, are responsible for making me that hard. I. Want. You."

"For now," I amended.

"Forever. I have made you my chosen. I can't undo that."

"You won't want me when I am all gray and wrinkly."

"Try me."

Damn I was tempted. "You're a vampire," I said feebly.

"I am also a man, or shall I show you?"

"No, I think I can do without show and tell."

"Are you a virgin and just nervous?"

"Are you?" I asked blushing.

"Really? You're going to ask me that question? No, my dear I am not. Now answer."

"Of course, not"

"I plan on seducing you and what you should do is just lay back and enjoy it. You know you want to."

I caught my breath and was suddenly nervous. I technically wasn't a virgin, but it had only been the one time and it was painful and unexciting. It was a huge disappointment.

"Stop overthinking, you will enjoy it, I promise."

He was kissing me again and all thought left me. Thought returned sharply when his mouth closed over my right nipple and he sucked. I moaned and nearly fell off the bed. Shit that felt good. He lifted his head, "I gather that met your approval?"

"Yes." I said breathlessly.

"Are you sure? I'd hate to do anything you don't like." He was grinning at me.

"Shut up and do it again." He laughed wickedly and did it again, this time to my left nipple. When he stroked my right nipple with his thumb while sucking the left, I arched my back again and nearly levitated again. I hear him laugh wickedly.

"Methinks you liked that."

I groaned and was just a little annoyed by his arrogance. "Is that the best you can do?"

He arched an eyebrow up. "Did you seriously just challenge me?"

"Take it as you wish."

"Game on."

It didn't take long to realize how much out of my element I was. When he inserted a finger (or was that two?) and rubbed my clitoris with the pad of his thumb, I heard a loud moan and realized it was from me. I cringed just a bit from fear someone would walk in and catch us at it. "You keep looking at the door. Nobody is going to save you from this." I flushed but couldn't retort. I was wound too tightly and getting tighter with each movement of his thumb.

"Let go Allison. I can feel you want to."

I didn't think I could bear anymore and attempted to squirm. He kept me still and then I shattered. His thumb stopped briefly as he looked down at me thoughtfully.

"I don't know, Allison. I think I can do better than that."

I shattered again within seconds. I tried to say, "Wow," and I was pretty sure he heard me because he grinned before sending me on my way to another orgasm. He stopped and pinned my hands above my head and kissed me again. It was slow and thorough. When he pulled back, I noticed the scar just over his heart.

"How did you get that scar?"

"Someone was trying to kill me. They used silver."

"Will it fade?"

"Not likely. It has been that way for over two hundred years."

I was silent as I gathered up the courage to be bold and daring. "Can I touch it?"

"Of course, but you don't need to ask. Just saving my life earned you the right to touch me anywhere you like."

"Anywhere?" I eyed the waistband of his pants.

"Anywhere but be careful. Some areas will have consequences."

"Well I certainly hope they do."

My hands travelled down his chest to the buttons of his pants. In movies and books, unbuttoning a man's pants looks so easy but in reality, it can be awkward and not that smoothly done." He was amused as I muttered curses under my breath. "Do you need some help?"

"No," as I freed the last button. "Are you going to be capable? You're after all several hundred years old."

"I've been doing this for a few hundred years. Not only am I capable, I am actually pretty good at it. At least I've not had anyone complain."

"Good. Prove it."

I shoved his pants down and gasped. "Problem?" He asked amused.

"Nooo…. it's just there's quite a bit of you, isn't there?"

"I gather you haven't seen many?"

"Not up close and personal." He laughed again.

"You'll love it."

He kissed me again. I could feel him pushing at my entrance. A little of him inside then with each back and forth movement a little more.

"You're incredibly tight."

"Eventually, he stopped. I felt stretched and full. He reached up and caressed my cheek.

"See darling, I fit."

I was going to say something, but he moved, and I was left gasping clinking to the sheets. I had my ah-ha moment that this was why sex was popular. I lost count of my orgasms and was exhausted when Renaldo trembled and reached his orgasm.

He pulled me close and I laid my head on his chest. I whispered the only word I could. "Wow." I could feel him laughing but I didn't care. I closed my eyes and fell asleep.

Chapter Thirty-One – Allison

I dreamed I was on the porch of a cabin in the mountains. The view was beautiful, and I could hear the water of a nearby stream bubbling happily. An old woman with a long thick braid down her back with a walking stick opened the screen door.

"Welcome dearie."

"Who are you and where am I?"

"I am your great-grandmother, and this is my place. Or at least it was my place. As for where this is all in your dreams. You can call me Granny."

She made a come in motion with her free hand and I walked into the room where I gasped. "Papa?"

"Yes, it's me."

"It was awful! I saw you on tv. Why did you do such a stupid thing! Don't you know how many people you hurt?"

"Well I didn't really have a lot of choices. I was never going to survive that scandal and it was better this way. Besides it is only the physical. My soul allows visitations in the dream world apparently."

"Of course, it does," said the bitter voice of Cassandra at the door.

"I would think you would be happy. I am out of the way."

"Yes and no. There is a reason why Granny and you are here together. Why?"

I was annoyed. "Can't you give him a break? Even in his death you must hate him?"

Cassandra was going to say something, but Granny interjected, "She's is right, Cassandra. It's time to let go."

"You're taking sides?" Cassandra asked incredulously.

"No, but it is pointless and a waste of time. Now sit down as we only have so much time."

I was amazed when Cassandra sat down without a word.

"You know what you are now, Cassandra?"

"Yes, Morrigan."

"What's Morrigan?" I asked.

"You are. She'll explain when you are awake."

"She better," I muttered.

"There is a third." My father blurted out.

"Third what?"

"Sister. There has to be. Morrigan comes in three."

I saw down stunned. Cassandra however had plenty to say. "Couldn't you have kept it in your britches? Where is she?"

"I don't know. Until I died, I had no idea but if I gave life to two Morrigan, there is a third."

"And do you at least remember who all you have fucked?"

"Language, Cassandra, language," Granny said sharply.

"Of course, I know who all I have fucked. Her name is Andrea Thompson. It has to be her kid. She was after Allison's mother. I insisted on a paternity. The results came back as not mine. How she managed to pull it off, I don't know. She disappeared after that."

"Awesome. A needle in a haystack."

"Renaldo could find out."

"Renaldo the Vampire King of Chicago, Renaldo? My great-grandmother asked sharply.

"Yes that one. Why?"

"Apparently, he has made Allison his chosen," Cassandra said with a tone of resignation in her voice, "Also he is the first Rat King in over a thousand years. Appropriate isn't it?"

"Our time is running out. This is important. If there is a third, it will wake up. It's already starting to wake up. I can feel it stirring."

"It?" I asked.

"Nightmares."

They were fading, "I cried for you, Daddy." Cassandra shouted.

"I am so sorry for what I did to you."

They were gone and Cassandra buried her face in her hands.

I went over to her and put my arms around her. The world dissolved and I woke up. I gasped, "I need to get dressed now!"

Renaldo arched an eyebrow. "But I rather like you this way."

"Cassandra is on her way to our rooms."

"You know this how?"

"We had a dream."

"You dreamed she would be coming."

"No but she will. I don't think she is going to take seeing me naked in bed with you to well."

He wisely threw my clothes towards me. "I know it sounds insane. Oh, and could you help me find my sister?"

"Isn't she about to barge in?"

"No, apparently there is another one."

"And you found this out how?"

"Dream. My father told me."

The phone began to ring. Renaldo picked up. "I understand. Let's not have her barge in. Instead let me arrange breakfast. It will give Allison time to shower or take a bath."

He turned around after he hung up. "She isn't going to barge in. You are going to take a shower and we are all going to meet where you and she will be served breakfast."

I reluctantly padded to the bathroom. The urgency got to me. "It will wake up." It sounded so ominous. It made me hope I didn't have another sister, but I suspected I did.

Chapter Thirty-Two – Julie

I could hear the scurrying of my mother around the house with her cronies. There was an edge of panic in her voice. Something was going on. I knew she would be opening the door to the room that she had me hidden behind soon. I nudged the little dog in my lap. "It's time to go back Fluffy."

Fluffy jumped down from my lap and looked at me with those sad eyes that got sadder each time she was summoned. She melted into the earth below just as the door opened. When that door opened was the only light I would see. I missed the sunlight, but I didn't mind the darkness. Someone would be afraid of the Darkness, but they didn't know what I did. She didn't know what I knew. By the time my mother reached the bottom there wasn't even a trace of my dog.

I got up hastily. She looked me up and down and said, "Well that explains everything." A very cryptic statement but I had learned not to say anything back. She sat down a bowl of some sort of soup for me to eat. If she was going to go on a rant, she would do it regardless of whether I said anything or not. Surprisingly she didn't and slammed back up the stairs.

I paid a lot closer attention to what was being said but it didn't really make sense because it was about Cassandra James and that she was the supposedly dead daughter of the Reverend Monroe. I bet that ticked my mother off. She was a follower of his. She absolutely loved his work. Then I heard "She's got to die."

The problem was that I didn't want to die. I wanted to live. No, the darkness was meant to be a punishment, but I was never alone. Not as long as I could raise Fluffy. I promised myself this. If I could survive this, I'd leave Fluffy alone. She liked where she would go and didn't really want to come back. She came back because I could make her. My poor Fluffy. As terrible as I felt though, the loneliness that would make this unbearable was worse. I wanted to cry but I wouldn't let myself. If I showed weakness, I'd not be able to survive.

I finished my soup because food was not a commodity I could waste. As soon as I took that last bite though I realized I had made a serious mistake because my head was swimming and I was suddenly very drowsy. That funny taste wasn't cheaper than store brand soup. After holding me captive since I graduated high school, she finally decided to kill me after all. I wonder why she had the gumption to do it now and not sooner. What was it that I ingested? Was it a poison or was it something that would make it impossible for me to defend myself which I always intended even if I had to raise every dead thing in the city to survive? I tried to raise Fluffy so that I could at least have my beloved dog to myself, but I was too sleepy to even do that. I was going to die alone and it singularly sucked.

Chapter Thirty-Three – Renaldo

When Allison had gone into the shower, I closed my eyes and reached out to Jared.

"What the fuck is going on Jared?"

"I will tell you at breakfast lad."

"Allison woke up ranting about a dream."

"I know. Cassandra too. What I do know is that those dreams are real."

"She asked me to help find a sister."

"Cassandra says there may be one. It makes sense now that I think about it."

"But she claims it was her father that told her."

"Your chosen is not your average woman. I do know this. If there is a third, she is as powerful and needs to be found."

"Swear you will explain everything at breakfast."

"I swear. Allison is going to need you. I have been meaning to tell you sooner, but things got in the way."

I hated that there were secrets and I was in the dark. Yet as I sat at the breakfast table with two beautiful red-headed women stuffing themselves like they haven't eaten and Jared calmly telling the most improbable story, I think I would have preferred my ignorance.

"Legend has it that the Goddess fell in love with a mortal man and they had quite a lot of sex. The results were predictable, and she got pregnant. They had three daughters. Some say they were triplets. Some say it was three pregnancies. Over the centuries the story has changed, and that Goddess really is three, the maiden, the crone, and the mother. No matter the mythology Cassandra's great-grandmother believes they are direct descendants and that one day the Morrigan would appear again. Signs of the Morrigan were handed down for centuries. Cassandra and from observation Allison fit them. If there are two from the Reverend, then the chances of the third are very much a reality."

I sat down after pacing. I sighed and said, "I don't suppose there is a name to go by?"

"Andrea Thompson," Cassandra replied in unison with Allison.

"I am sure she was a member of the church. Papa picked my mother from the church."

Jared snorted at that.

"Would there be public records?" I asked feeling if there weren't this would be almost impossible.

"Yes." Allison said with confidence.

"Really?" Cassandra asked. "He was notorious about privacy."

"He was but he did keep a record of members for accounting purposes. But they are heavily encrypted," Allison explained.

"I'm pretty sure I can find someone who can hack the system," I said confidently. In fact, I could think of at least 3 hackers that I worked with and then there was my untapped rodent network. Stunned I had the database in under an hour because one of my rats just happened to be former CIA and was part of the team that kept tabs on the good reverend. All I had to do was explain that there might be another heir to his estate.

It took very little more digging to match the daughter to the records. It seemed like her father liked to cheat every two to three years. With Cassandra being 26, Allison at 23, and Julie at 20. The only problem is that Julie disappeared after high school. Nobody's seen or heard from her. There was a police report filed with her missing by someone who was a friend, but it was dismissed.

"Something doesn't feel right," Allison said, and Cassandra agreed. Within minutes we were planning on paying Julie's mother a visit.

Chapter Thirty-Four – Cassandra

If someone told me that I was going to be on an airplane to Miami with Jared, Renaldo, and sister looking for another sister a month ago, I would have called it bullshit. Yet that is exactly what I found myself doing. Once we landed in Miami, Jared went looking for the person who filed the missing person's report, and Renaldo, myself, and Allison decided to visit the last address of Julie's mother.

The house had all the curtains drawn and if it were not for the car in the driveway, you would think that nobody was home. We rang the doorbell, which was one of those doorbell cameras and knocked but nobody came to the door. Renaldo, however, could hear movement in the house and

"You might as well answer the door. I'll just have it kicked in," he shouted.

Finally, the door lock was turned, and the door opened. A woman with grey hair that looked like what Granny would say was rode hard and put wet stood there. "What do you want?"

"We're looking for Andrea Thompson. Does she still live at this address?"

"I am she."

"Miss Thompson, we are investigating the disappearance of your daughter Julie."

"I don't know where she is."

She tried to slam the door, but Renaldo stopped it. Annoyance and anger flashed across the face of Andrea. "I could call the cops."

"But you won't," Allison said calmly. "If you called the cops, they would have to search the premises. As I am sure you recognize this is Cassandra James. Cassandra is the world's premiere paranormal investigator. If she thinks you have somehow have someone imprisoned don't you think they are going to look? Now you need to tell us where Julie is."

"I don't know."

I knew the woman was lying because it felt like a lie. Allison, however, shocked me when she slapped the woman hard and pushed past her. She surprised Renaldo too apparently. His eyebrows shot up and murmured "Well this is how we're going to do it then." She walked through the house and out the back door where there was a shed. She opened the shed that had a coffin to the side and hole dug for it. It didn't take a genius to figure out what was going on. My heart stopped as the fear that we were too late for our sister.

"Please! Please don't be dead," Allison shouted frantically as she was trying desperately to open the coffin lid. Finally, she angrily pointed at it, "Open damn you."

Much to my shock, and probably Allison's as well the lid flew off, nails and all. As shocked as I was didn't rival the look of astonishment on Renaldo's face though. "Well that was impressive," he said keeping his voice casual. "Is she dead, Ren?" I barely was able to speak around the lump that had formed in my throat.

He touched the girl in the coffin. "No. Her heart still beats but it's weak. Help is on the way."

"How?" I asked.

"Rat king, here." Who knew he was going to prove so useful.

"Where is her mother?"

"Bruno is taking care of the hag."

"What?!?" I said alarmed as I knew that taking care of someone could mean something quite permanent.

"Relax Cassandra. Poor choice of words. He is tying her up. Though if you want, I could make her disappear."

"Don't tempt me. Let's work on saving Julie's life."

"Cass?" I cringed. Allison started calling me that after the dream and I couldn't get her to stop. Renaldo on the other hand found it hilarious.

"Yes?"

"I need you to hold her other hand. She is drawing energy from me. If she gets from us both maybe it will help."

Allison was right. Julie was fighting hard to survive. With the immediate danger over I took an assessment of Julie. She had similar features that were like me and Allison, but her hair appeared to be black though it was so filthy it could be lighter. It did make her skin look almost translucent, at least the portions that didn't have bruises. I didn't even want to think about what would have happened if our father hadn't killed himself. We would never have known she even could have existed. She would have died a horrible death in obscurity.

If she healed like Allison and I, the level of abuse she had to live with had been tremendous. If she disappeared two years ago after graduation, then she must have been all alone for those two years dealing with it. It didn't make me feel very fond of my father for somehow not knowing about her existence.

When the sound of the ambulance got near, Renaldo reached in and picked her up, cradling him to his chest. He carried her out as the ambulance pulled in and laid her gently on the gurney.

She was extremely skinny and obviously malnourished. One of the paramedics was a rat apparently. He crossed himself and muttered, "Dios," fervently when he saw her.

I turned and unfortunately saw her mother with Bruno holding her struggling form. I found myself walking over to her and much to the surprise of Bruno, I hit the woman in the face as hard as I could. My hand hurt from the impact, but it was worth it as I saw her crumple to the ground. When I turned, Allison, I shrugged, "That's how you hit someone who really deserves it."

She raised an eyebrow and said, "Thank you for the lesson. Do you feel better?"

"Lots," I said truthfully.

"Good. You're riding with Julie to the hospital in the ambulance. It might not be a good idea to leave you behind while they sort her mother out. Jared will meet you there. I'll be there shortly with Renaldo."

My last glimpse of Allison was with Renaldo behind her, holding her. I looked down at the girl and said firmly, "You are not allowed to get involved with someone as disreputable as Renaldo."

I was startled when I faint voice whispered, "I'll do my best."

Jared was waiting when we arrived. A man standing next to him looked very familiar. "It's an honor. I'll be looking after Julie. Does she heal like you?"

I was started and then I looked at him closer. "Dr. Wolfe?"

"You remember," he said with relief.

"How could I ever forget?" I threw my arms around him much to the surprise of Jared. I looked over at Jared and explained, "Dr. Wolfe was the one who helped me after I escaped."

Jared was tactful not to mention that I never mentioned him. I was a little uncomfortable. I never forgot but it was difficult for me to discuss my childhood sometimes. I changed the subject and Jared, bless him, let me. "I don't know if she heals like me but given I and my other sister do, it is a reasonable expectation."

"Then I will play it by ear. Forgive me, but I have a patient to care for."

When he was gone, Jared raised an eyebrow, "He saw you after you escaped?"

"Literally. When I escaped, he was the first doctor on the scene. He covered me because I was n-naked."

"You don't have to talk about it. I just didn't think of someone having known you right after for some reason."

I smiled. "No, it's okay. I just didn't think I would ever see him again."

It was over an hour of waiting. Allison showed up with Renaldo and we were taken to a private waiting area because the media was now alerted to our presence being in Miami. Finally, a nurse came in and let me know that one of us could come in. Being the eldest I got picked.

When I walked in, she was awake and responding to the doctor though she was groggy. I felt immense relief and had to blink back tears.

Chapter Thirty-Five - Julie

I woke to the sterile smell of a doctor's office or maybe a hospital. I began to assess myself from head to toe for any injuries as I put things together. Somehow, I had been rescued. A doctor had scurried in and said, "Oh good. You're awake. I'm Dr. Wolfe."

I snorted to that. He reeked of being a shapeshifter and thought how appropriately he was named.
"How did I get found?"

"That is a story for Cassandra to tell you?"

"Cassandra?" I had dreamed I thought that the Cassandra James had rescued a nobody like me but that was merely a dream wasn't it?

"Yes. Cassandra James."

"I must be dead or still dreaming. If I'm dead the afterlife isn't all that bad, I guess. If I'm dreaming, don't wake me up please."

"No, not dead or dreaming," said a dry voice.

She stepped forward and a rush of affection filled me for this woman who quite literally saved my life. I had only ever seen her image on tv, but she looked different. Perhaps because I thought she must be 7 feet tall for what she has done for the monster community.

"I don't understand. Why of all the people in the world that you chose to save me?"

"You will. Apparently, your mother and my father got together, and those extra Bible lessons produced you."

"Ah you know who my father is then? She would never tell me."

"Yes. He is the illustrious and filthy hypocrite Reverend James Monroe."

"The leader of Humans Only?"

"The very one."

"Does he know about me?"

He honestly didn't know about you. I suspect your mother knew something about me and cut ties with him.

I snorted. He was married. Why her mother would be shocked that he had other by blows was beyond me. When I express it, Cassandra smiled gently.

"I'm not illegitimate," and waited patiently.

I wrapped my brain on what I knew of the man which was a fair bit. My mother thought he walked on water. He had no children other than apparently me and Cassandra. He had a daughter, but she died.

"His biography says no living children by his wife."

"His biography was correct as far as the world knew for quite some time. I was born Allyssa Monroe."

"If that is true that must be very, very inconvenient for him because she was supposed to have been killed by vampires."

"I am not lying and yes it was very inconvenient for him. He admitted the truth publicly. Just before he killed himself on national television."

"Where did you go then? Why tell such a huge lie?"

"He handed me over to a priest to get the sing out of me. I was captive for over 100 nights where I was captive for a hundred nights where I was brutally tortured before I was able to escape.

Ironically, I ended up in this hospital and the doctor attending you happened to be on the street when I emerged from my captivity naked and covered in blood and filth."

It was a lot to take in, so I changed the subject.

"Who was the vampire? The one who touched me?"

I watched her blink for a second. "How did you know a vampire touched you?"

"I have an affinity for dead things. My mother had a problem with it."

"The vampire that touched you was Renaldo, the Vampire King of Chicago."

"Don't you two dislike each other?"

"It's complicated. I will explain it all to you later but for now Dr. Wolfe needs to examine you."

"There was you, the vampire, and a rat. Who was the other person?"

Again, I surprised Cassandra which kind of was nifty. "Allison. She is your sister as well. Our father seemed to have an ability to keep his dick to himself." She smiled brightly and walked out.

Dr. Wolfe worked efficiently. He finally stopped and assessed me. "Mostly you are fine. What I worry is getting you back onto a regular diet. You're very thin and malnourished.

"I know. Meals were not very regular."

"I'm not going to put a feeding tube in just yet. I think you will be fine with access to food. I don't want you to go crazy and eat a bunch of junk food. That won't help the problem and you're to eat something every two to three hours Once you gain a good ten pounds or so you're to start an exercise program to build muscle."

"What will become of me?" I blurted out and blushed for interrupting him.

You have one sister who is the chosen to the vampire king of Charlotte. You have another who is the chosen of the Vampire King of Chicago. You have an amazing will to live. I imagine what will become of you will be completely up to you."

Chapter Thirty-Six -- Alison

Even though Cassandra had seen Julie I was happy when the doctor was done, and we could both go and see her. I had glanced at her while she was in that coffin. She seemed cheerful enough though a bit wary. We were all kind of feeling each other out. Growing up as only children made us all more self-contained and we didn't want to step on the toes of the others.

Cassandra though was as usual her very direct self. "When you told me earlier that you had an affinity for the dead what exactly does that mean?"

I can raise the dead."

"Like Zombies?" I asked fascinated.

"Kind of. My zombies are much better looking than the ones you see."

"How long have you been able to do it?'

"Since I was about 8 or 9. I didn't get caught at it until I was around 14 years old. That's when things changed for me."

"I'm not understanding," Cassandra said. "Are you telling me you do it without any form of a ritual?"

"That would be correct. I've never heard of anything like me."

"Because there isn't. What you're doing is kind of like necromancy."

At this point Cassandra explained everything to Julie who became more and more astonished. "I'd like for you to come live with me at The Endless Night. From there you can heal and figure out what the next steps will be for you."

"Only on one condition. I need to get Fluffy."

"Fluffy?"

"She's my dog. I know that you are waiting for me to be all damaged, but I wasn't alone. I raised my dog on a regular basis. She kept me company. I promised her that if I got free that I would find her a better resting place."

Cassandra smiled and then started laughing.

"Are you okay Cass?" I asked concerned.

"Just fine. I just had a mental image."

"Of what?"

"Of Jared and Renaldo digging for a grave before finding out what she can do."

Even my mouth twitched at the image. "It would be an improving program for Ren." I said grinning.

"Would you do it?" I asked Julie. "Allow our respected chosen's dig before revealing yourself.

She smiled shyly and said "Absolutely."

Chapter Thirty-Seven – Julie

Meeting Jared was fascinating. I had never met a vampire before so for me to be able to identify one touching me and to meeting one was actually pretty thrilling to me. There was a familiarity of their energy to that of those I raise from the dead. In fact, it was very similar but not quite the same. I was pretty sure that I couldn't call a vampire like Jared or Renaldo to me. I wouldn't make any wagers that with a vampire less powerful I couldn't.

He argued with me over going back to the house which I insisted. I was adamant and he was very badly outnumbered. Renaldo wasn't thrilled either about digging up a corpse of a beloved pet, but he sided with Allison for self-preservation. I loved how they assumed they would be digging. Cassandra and Allison knew better and for some perverse reason let them remain deluded.

We got there with the shovels. When asked where to start digging, I pointed vaguely to a spot. As they started digging, I asked Cassandra and Allison, "How long do you plan on watching them dig?"

"Oh, not to terribly long. Maybe two feet?" Cassandra said.

"Or three," said Allison with a twinkle in her eyes.

"You just want to see if Renaldo will take his shirt off after a while," Cassandra accused.

"Well there is that. Plus, this is part of his improvement plan."

I laughed and realized it was the first time since I had laughed in years. I met the boy that I went to school with that reported me missing to the police to thank him. It was quite awkward, but he deserved thanks for it because it helped Cassandra find me. Renaldo looked back and glared at me. "If you like you could help."

"You're right. I could. Stand back and let me show you how a pro does it." I let that part of me that I hold back go and I whistled, "Fluffy! Come to me girl!"

She exploded out of the earth in a joy she hadn't shown in years. She ran a lap around the yard as the two astonished vampires looked on. She ran to me and launched herself into my arms. "I'm free girl," I said laughing as she licked my face. I looked at the two vampires, "We can go now."

When we got into the limo, Fluff jumped into the arms of Jared who examined her thoroughly. "I've heard stories about necromancers. It's a very rare gift."

I shrugged. "I guess. I've always had it. I thought others could call the dead."

"No, you truly raise the dead. Don't be confused with animators. What they do is raise a body and make it work. The body is at the mercy of the animator. Much like a puppet at the mercy of its puppeteer. I assume all of Fluffy's original soul and personality are there?"

"Yes."

"What happens if you don't call the dead?"

"Accidents can happen. It really was a risk my mother took by imprisoning me. She thought chaining me with chains with silver in them would stop me and that it was successful. What I really did was raise Fluffy night after night. You see why I couldn't just leave her there."

"What kind of accidents?"

"When I was trying to suppress it and keep it hidden from them, I accidentally raised the cemetery down the road."

Cassandra looked astonished, "There's got to be at least 100 graves."

"151 to be exact. I didn't know I had done it until one of the residents of the cemetery came knocking on our door looking for me. He liked where he went and wanted to go back. I think you can appreciate how upset my mother was to be getting me out of bed and driving me to the cemetery at 3am. It took almost an hour to sort it out too."

"How can you tell zombie from real?" Allison asked.

"Fluffy will start to degrade after about a week above ground. She doesn't like it very much at all."

Jared finally spoke, "Can you control a vampire?"

I looked at him helplessly, "I don't know."

I heard Cassandra draw a deep breath in.

"I know I wouldn't be able to call either you or Renaldo. You're both very strong but one that isn't strong? I couldn't really say for sure."

We were all very silent. Jared finally spoke, "I need to make inquiries among the old vampire community about necromancers. My maker told me that necromancers were a danger and should be executed immediately and even that isn't a guarantee of killing a necromancer. As far as I know he only ever told me. I believe he only mentioned it because I asked about someone historical that he encountered. He didn't end very well either.

"What happened to him?"

"He was crucified and a few days later escaped his tomb. He was Jesus of Nazareth. He recognized Jesus based on what his maker told him of one but that would have gone back almost five or six thousand years. I was under the distinct impression his maker preferred to forget about it and given my maker killed his shortly after I don't know who all knows. I am very old myself as a vampire and I'm the only surviving vampire that he made. The older vampires weren't very nice to those they created and so there was a fair bit of makers getting killed by those they made."

"How did you survive then?"

"I treated those I made better and I must admit I factor self-preservation in when I make a vampire."

I laughed at that. Again, a true laugh. It sounded almost foreign to me. It was a good foreign.

Chapter Thirty-Eight -- Allison

It took nearly a month longer than anyone planned for us to get back home to The Ivory Tower. All of my things had been moved into Renaldo's rooms. Julie was definitely our sister and it was fascinating to see her raise the dead like she could.

Much to Jared's profound relief he tested her against new vampires, and she couldn't make them do her bidding. Many did want to do her bidding but only because she was likeable which may be a separate kind of magic.

Renaldo by the time we got back to Chicago was fully comfortable in his role as The Rat King. He let it be known that he was breaking his organization up and if anyone had an issue there wasn't a place in the world that they could go to that he wouldn't know about any plots.

Cassandra moved into The Endless Night permanently and everything seemed to be well. As for me, I couldn't have been happier. Ren left me in charge of his PR campaign so I could figure out how best to humiliate him to improve his image during the day. At night…. well you know."

The End

Ground Zero: The First Zombie Attack

Duchess MacKinnon

PART I

John Doyle was a miserable piece of shit and everyone in the village of Spellingworth, Wales knew it. He was a foul-mouthed bastard that if it was just the fact that he couldn't string two sentences together without saying the word "Fuck" that would be almost manageable. No, he was temperamental and abusive. Everyone felt sorry for his wife because they heard him openly verbally abuse her in public many a time. Often when she had to get his drunk ass from the pub.

Some drunks are happy drunks. He was not a happy drunk. He was a mean one who had a taste for the ladies and while he thought he was something to look at, he was rather repulsive with his teeth rotting from the alcohol he drank. He loved to pinch the barmaids when they passed by and they all learned never to turn their back to him. Heaven help a bar maid who gave him a set down. The last one ended up in tears and had to go to another pub because he called her a fucking moronic twat and that was the milder things he said. He went on and on about her for almost an hour until the pub owner had to come in and gently make him go home.

Then there was the strange new girl. She had the misfortune to serve him since none of the others would and because she was new the other bar maids decided not to warn her. When her back was turned, he reached over and grabbed her between the legs. She straightened and one had to admire her dignity as she said, "If you don't release me, you'll be very sorry."

That enraged him because how dare she embarrass him in public. He called her a slut and then some and stumbled his way home muttering about how women were nothing but bitches. The new girl whom nobody seemed to know her name quit and the pub owner knowing what he was quietly gave her wages and let her go on.

So, in short, poor John Doyle was loathed, despised, and even hated by everyone from his wife and children to everyone else. His only claim to friends were those who were online, and he didn't even keep them long because he would spoil them with his drunken ranting. You almost had to feel sorry for him. He had after all fought for his country and served with honors in the army.

What he didn't realize is that he grabbed the wrong woman and that he just sat forth the warning shot that nobody heard. Something that was going to transcend two continents and he was going to be ground zero.

After leaving the pub he stumbled home. The entire time he couldn't shake the feeling that eyes were watching him. He knew when he was being watched because he didn't survive the army for nothing. He bellowed, "Alright you miserable bastard. Show yerself. You can 't fool me. I know you're a watching meself."

When John got home from his pub, he flung himself into his easy chair. Next to it was a brand-new crate of his favorite beer. He reached over and grabbed one. As he cracked it opened and savored that first glorious swig it occurred to him that if he laid off the drink, he might actually feel better. He knew people thought he had a problem, but he could stop drinking anytime he wanted. He was the type that could take it or leave it.

He heard a noise in the kitchen but dismissed it as his wife ratting about. She must have forgotten to take something out for supper the next day. No if he laid off the drink, he'd be awake for breakfast so in reality he was helping her by reducing one meal a day for her to cook for him. Then it occurred to him that whatever was going on in the kitchen couldn't be Dora. She was staying the night at her sisters so she could get to work early. Now that was the perfect woman he thought. She knew her place most of the time. As a bonus she earned her own keep and still had dinner on the table. She would occasionally step out of line but nothing a good shake or slap didn't cure. He owed those lapses in judgement to the bitches she worked with.

If it wasn't her in the kitchen who the hell was it in there? Grumbling he got up and went to the rifle hanging on the wall and headed to kitchen. He wasn't very far in when something lunged at him and knocked him down. He felt a searing pain on his right wrist. It wasn't until he felt wetness that he realized he had been bitten and that whatever bit him would take another bite if he wasn't fast enough.

It was dark in the kitchen as he wrestled about to get it off him. He couldn't figure out what kind of animal had gotten into the house. Whatever it was, it was big. He was grappling around until he knocked over a rack and realized it was the fireplace accessories rack. He grabbed for the only weapon he could find in the dark and jabbed it backwards getting a satisfying oof. He scrambled onto his feet and swung it for all it was worth as it was going to lunge and again and got a very satisfying thud. He stepped quickly out of the way and flipped the light on so he could see what he was dealing with.

He was shocked to the core when he saw it was a woman. A very disheveled looking woman but it was a woman who bit him. She stank and her clothes were ripped and filthy. Though at one time they were very nice clothes. He had heard about those bath salts as the newest drug and wondered if she was one of those.

He was able to get his rifle as she struggled to get up. When she got up, he noticed something was wrong with her eyes. The best word he could come up with is blank. They were dead eyes. He almost dropped his rifle again.

"Hey now. Don't do anything you'll regret."

She started towards him. "I will shoot. I have the right to defend meself in me own home!" She continued to him when he finally with a sigh allowed his training to take over and he shot her. It took 12 rounds to get her to stop moving. Once she stopped moving, he took a good look at her face trying to place it because she looked familiar. Horror dawned on him when he realized who it was. Her name was Amelia Pendleton.

The problem was that Amelia Pendleton was supposed to be six feet under. She died a week ago in a car accident. An accident in which he may have been responsible for. She lost control of her car, went off the road, and flipped three times. The reason she lost control was she was trying to avoid hitting him because he had dozed off and woke only when he thought someone shouted, "John! Wake the fuck up!"

His arm was throbbing, so his thinking was not all that clear. If it had been. If he had drank less. If he had been a better man, he would have asked a very important question. If Amelia Pendleton had died last week, how did her bullet riddled corpse end up lying in his kitchen?

His arm hurt as if he been bitten a 2nd or 3rd time. He unwrapped his makeshift bandage and vomited until there was nothing left in his stomach. He had seen everything in the Army, so he always prided himself on his constitution. However, this sight really got to him. Half his hand was gone, and he could see his flesh simply dissolve in front of his eyes and it was spreading up his arm.

He always said that only two things spewed venom: A snake and a woman. So, in his drunken panicked mind it stood to reason her bite was truly venomous but who would have an antidote for women's venom? He could well imagine being laughed at when he called 999. No antidote and being humiliated…. He determined the next logical choice was the arm would have to come off.

He stumbled over to the liquor cabinet because this was going to require the hard stuff and grabbed a bottle of Jack Daniels No. 7 and took 2 healthy swigs. It should probably be noted that a healthy swig for him was upending the bottle and chugging a few times. He grabbed several towels from the linen closet and made his way to the garage.

As it just so happened, he had bought himself a brand-new power saw that he hadn't used so he knew two things: It was clean, and it would get the job done. He might even be able to explain it all away with a little accident. He tied himself a good tourniquet just above his elbow, took a couple of more healthy swigs from his friend Jack for courage, murmured "God Save The Queen," and flipped the switch. After some pain that made his swear, "Holy Fuck Mother of God" he heard a meaty sound hit the ground. Almost like the sound when you drop a hamburger patty in the kitchen floor by mistake. He quickly wrapped the stump of his arm in several of his wife's thickest towels. He was sure he would catch hell when she must burn them because of all the blood staining them.

He watched dispassionately as the remains of his arm slowly disappeared before his eyes. Almost as if acid was dissolving it into nothingness. His wife was never going to believe him. Except for the body. Christ! The Body! He couldn't let his wife see that. He sighed with resignation that he was going to have to get rid of it. Fortunately, he had a lake behind the house. He was simply going to drag it there and dump her in. He stumbled back into the kitchen where he left but it was gone. Where the hell was it? "Well damn me," he muttered. "I seem to have misplaced the body." Never of course thinking that if it crawled out a grave to attack him, even if he put 12 shots into it, that it wouldn't get up and take itself off again. Logic was not one of his strong points.

He walked back into the living room and sat heavily down in the recliner. He glanced down at the heavily wrapped stump of his arm to make sure it wasn't bleeding all over everything. He was going to have to go seek medical attention soon, but he needed to rest for a few minutes first. He was dizzy from losing so much blood and oddly he felt pins and needles all over his body but paid it no attention assuming blood loss and the Jack would be causing it.

Then he heard the screen door creak open and almost mesmerized he watched the doorknob turn and the front door slowly open. The barmaid from earlier walked in. Unable to help himself, "What? Came back for another grab? Liked it did ya?"

"Not really," she said. "I just came by to collect your head.

"Oh, is that what they call a blow job these days? Collecting head."

"No, no. Poor delusional John. You haven't figured it out, have you? Well I suppose not. They never do."

"Figured out what, bitch?"

"You are a dead man. Miss Pendleton's bite? You figured out it was toxic I see."

John held up the stump of his arm. "I cut it off," he laughed with glee.

"I know. It's already began. Don't you feel weird?"

As a matter of a fact he did feel strange.

"I've never felt better, twat," he lied with bravado. "Now get yer skanky ass out of me house!"

"No. I don't think so. I'll just wait. It shouldn't be all that much longer." She calmly took a chair. He tried to get up to forcibly remove her, but he couldn't. The pins and needles got much worse rapidly and when he looked down, he began to scream. Blood had blossomed from his trousers, running down his legs into his shoes making them squishy. He kicked his shoes off and screamed in agony when his feet went with them at the ankles.

At that moment he was filled with hate and rage but helpless to express it except with screaming curses at the barmaid who just smiled calmly through it. The pain spread upwards to his groin. He stopped thinking at that point. Maybe even breathing. He couldn't be sure. All he could think about was the pain. It felt like he was being repeatedly kicked in the balls over and over again while being stabbed at the same time with a hot poker. He couldn't even writhe in pain.

The first rational thought he managed to come to as he adjusted to the pain was that he was going to die. He knew that. At least it would soon be over. He could lose only so many body parts and blood before the inevitable. Or at least that was what he thought. It was like a bonfire licking up his body. He screamed himself hoarse. It eventually occurred to him that it would never end but he dismissed that idea as literally impossible. It seemed like hours until finally he fell over and hit his head on the floor. It was the first moments though that he didn't feel agonizing pain. Was this death? That this was it?

The Barmaid lifted his head up. Her touch almost lovingly. He had no voice but that didn't stop him from mouthing curses and giving her a piece of his mind. She laughed with genuine amusement. Heavens he was fowl. "You're not very bright, are you? You'd think you would be attempting to get on my good side. Not remain on my bad side." She shrugged. "Well it doesn't really matter. You are only a small piece of a much bigger plan. The master will be pleased. I do so love a win/win. Your wife is free of you without the headache of a divorce. The pub is free of you. There will be barmaids that will sleep better knowing you are not present. Your children can sleep better without the fear of what you will do to their mother one day. You will never degrade another woman and you will have a very long time to think about it.

She could see the defiant puzzlement in his eyes. "I told you. I am here to collect your head. She then turned so he could see his dissolving headless body. She took immense joy in the horror in his eyes. His mouth working silent words.

Part II

Detective John Watson had it easy as his area didn't get a lot of crime. However, he'd worked for the police in London where he got more than his share of excitement. Today was one of those days he wished he was still back in London.

She was a pretty and small woman. Must not have been much taller than five feet if that. Her black hair was in a high ponytail and she was wearing black from head to toe. She was calm and disturbingly cheery. She was carrying a sack and announced, "I want to confess everything."

"Oh?"

"Yes. John Doyle reached between my legs and grabbed my you know what."

He snorted. Yeah that sounded like the man. He'd had a few encounters with him and had heard the rumors of him harassing the girls at the pub. None had come into make a confession or complaint though.

"Do you wish to file a complaint? We could bring him up on charges of sexual assault."

She walked over to his desk and sat calmly down.

"No. That won't be necessary," she said calmly, "He won't be doing it to anyone again. He's dead."

His heart sank as he envisioned the paperwork he had to file over the next hours. He steeled himself to ask the important question.

"How do you know that?"

"I chopped off his head and got rid of his body."

He really wished she had stopped there. He was pretty sure he was going to have nightmares for months from what she did next. She reached into the sack and plopped his head down onto the table. If It had been only that he would have been fine. But it was mouthing what seemed to be words. He commented on it. She shrugged and said, "Well it's said Mary, Queen of Scots mouth moved long after her head was separated from her body."

He arrested her and took her into custody. He sent the police to notify the wife which took some time since she apparently spent the night with her sister, and it was well verified. Which gave him at least some peace of mind because she was clearly not involved. Could she have been more demonstrative in her grief? Maybe. However, if he was bad to other women, he could only imagine what he was like to his loved ones.

Then his prisoner and the head simply disappeared. All the cameras were turned off for a period of almost half an hour, so nobody knew where she went. They organized a manhunt but just as she appeared and nobody really knew who she was, she also disappeared. She was put into the news cycle but that didn't yield any results. The only thing out of place was that his widow embraced her freedom and the life insurance she got with joy. However, given that she had endured his abuse he could understand why.

While the detective pondered the leads the barmaid was skipping down a stone pathway laughing. She was tossing up and catching what looked from a distance a ball, but it wasn't a ball. It was the head of John Doyle. He was no longer mouthing curses. Instead, permanently fixed upon his face was a look of a horror. As for his wife, freed from him she sold the house, took the money, and bought a lovely cottage in France just outside of Paris. She lived a very happy life after that.